THE MUSIC OF THE MONGOLS

EASTERN MONGOLIA

Da Capo Press Music Reprint Series
GENERAL EDITOR
FREDERICK FREEDMAN
VASSAR COLLEGE

THE MUSIC OF THE MONGOLS

EASTERN MONGOLIA

Collected by Henning Haslund-Christensen

Translation of Lyrics by K. Grønbech
Transcription of Music by Ernst Emsheimer

Preface by Sven Hedin

DA CAPO PRESS • NEW YORK • 1971

A Da Capo Press Reprint Edition

This Da Capo Press edition of *The Music of the Mongols: Eastern Mongolia* is an unabridged republication of the first edition published in Stockholm in 1943 as Publication 21 of the *Reports from the Scientific Expedition to the North-Western Provinces of China under the Leadership of Dr. Sven Hedin.*

Library of Congress Catalog Card Number 79-125045

SBN 306-70009-3

Published by Da Capo Press
A Division of Plenum Publishing Corporation
227 West 17th Street, New York, N.Y. 10011

Manufactured in the United States of America

THE MUSIC
of the
MONGOLS

A Mongol doing homage, to the accompaniment of musicians. To his right is a man performing on the *khil-khuur,* to his left another playing an instrument resembling the *dörwen-chikhe-khuur.* In the lower part of the picture two shawm-players and the newcomer's riding-horse; the camel symbolizes his caravan.

Drawn and painted by Lodai Lama of Jasaktu Khan in Khalkha Mongolia.

REPORTS FROM THE SCIENTIFIC EXPEDITION TO THE NORTH-WESTERN
PROVINCES OF CHINA UNDER THE LEADERSHIP OF DR. SVEN HEDIN
— THE SINO-SWEDISH EXPEDITION —
PUBLICATION 21

VIII. Ethnography
4

THE MUSIC OF THE MONGOLS

PART I

EASTERN MONGOLIA

PREFACE
by
SVEN HEDIN

ON THE TRAIL OF ANCIENT MONGOL TUNES
by
HENNING HASLUND-CHRISTENSEN

SPECIMENS OF MONGOLIAN POETRY
translated by
K. GRØNBECH

PRELIMINARY REMARKS ON MONGOLIAN MUSIC AND INSTRUMENTS
by
ERNST EMSHEIMER

MUSIC OF EASTERN MONGOLIA,
COLLECTED BY H. HASLUND-CHRISTENSEN,
noted down by
ERNST EMSHEIMER

STOCKHOLM 1943

Printed in Sweden

TRYCKERI AKTIEBOLAGET THULE

STOCKHOLM 1943

420975

C O N T E N T S

PREFACE

On introducing the Mongol songs collected by HENNING HASLUND-CHRISTENSEN in our series of scientific reports from the Swedish expeditions in Asia, I must first of all express my heart-felt thanks to the RASK-ØRSTED FOUNDATION in Copenhagen and its President, Professor N. E. NØRLUND, for their great generosity which has made it possible for us to publish a work the character and contents of which so greatly differ from the works hitherto supported by the Foundation.

It is my sincere hope that also the remaining musical material collected by HASLUND-CHRISTENSEN during the years 1928—1939 may subsequently be added to the present volume in our series. This work was startad in 1928 during the stay of the Sino-Swedish Expedition in Sinkiang. I well remember how after spending some time among the Qara-shahr Torguts HASLUND-CHRISTENSEN on his return to Urumchi in November of that year entertained us a whole night playing and singing the songs he had recorded on his little Edison phonograph. In my youth I had many a time listened to flutes and stringed instruments in the tent-villages of the Taijinär Mongols in Tsaidam, among the tribes in Alakshan, and when visiting the Khalkha people in Urga, and I had learnt to love the soft and dreamy strains and fascinating charm of the Mongol songs. But that November night in Urumchi the young Danish singer and I decided that it was to be his task in the expedition to collect and preserve as much as possible of the musical treasures of Mongolia as had not yet been obliterated by time or forgotten by the new generations. The present volume is thus only one in a series which we hope shortly to see continued in one or a couple of volumes. We think that in doing so we shall not only afford all friends of the Mongols and of Asia a pleasure, but that we may also and especially afford academic musical scientists an opportunity of studying the characteristics of Mongol music and comparing it with the songs and tunes of other Asiatic peoples. Even a layman like myself cannot very well escape noticing the great differences in the rhythm, passages and melody of the music of the various peoples of Asia. I have a vivid memory of the Persian orchestras which with their flutes, .trombones and drums every night bid the setting sun farewell from "nakara-khaneh", the drum-pavilion above the western city gate of Teheran, and every morning greeted the rising sun with their noisy music from the eastern gate. I remember the loud epic and erotic songs executed by the Kirghiz and the peoples of Eastern Turkistan to the accompaniment of flutes, two-stringed guitars and drums; the flute-playing of Arabs and bedouins with its slow dreamy charm; the bizarre tunes of the Tibetan begging friars produced on flutes made of the tibia of a nineteen-year-old girl and dual drums made of two human skulls. In the Far East I have often heard the noisy music and queer singing of the Chinese theatre and in Dai Nippon the wailing singing to the accompaniment of "koto" and the graceful dancing of the geishas.

But nevertheless I value the creations in which the Mongols have expressed their longing for musical harmony and lyric feeling higher than all these varied manifestations of Asiatic music on the human vocal chords or on instruments made by man. Consequently it gladdens my heart that thanks to the generosity of the RASK-ØRSTED FOUNDATION we are able to let people who have never been in Mongolia and who will probably never go there hear a living and true echo of the songs of the steppes and deserts.

All the necessary apparatus was most liberally placed at HASLUND'S disposal by A. B. RADIOTJÄNST, the Swedish Broadcasting Corporation, for which we offer our sincere thanks. All this equipment, and especially the instruments required in tracts lacking electricity, was elaborated by the Technical Department of Radiotjänst, and all costs were defrayed by that corporation, whose chief, Dr. ANDERS DYMLING, lent the plan his great enthusiasm and expert knowledge.

The musical treatment and the interpretation of the tunes recorded has been carried out with great care and skill by Dr. ERNST EMSHEIMER, Stockholm.

Dr. KAARE GRØNBECH, the greatest expert on Mongol languages in the North and a member of the Danish expedition of 1938—1939, has done the excellent translations of the Mongol texts in this book.

It is a pleasure for me to offer my sincere thanks to those gentlemen and to Dr. GÖSTA MONTELL, who has had the editor's arduous task and who has contributed to the illustrations of the work with several photographs. Most of the photographs were otherwise taken by Messrs. GRØNBECH and HASLUND-CHRISTENSEN, and thanks to the initiative of the latter the frontispiece was painted by LODAI LAMA, a Mongol emigrant from Khalkha to South Mongolia. It illustrates the Mongol conception of one of the songs.

Our gratitude is first of all due to the author and leader of the Danish expedition, Mr. HENNING HASLUND-CHRISTENSEN, a singer and a lover of music, to whom all credit is due for collecting and preserving the melodies and texts now published. The collection includes a number of Kalmuk songs recorded among some Volga Kalmuks that emigrated to Qara-shahr and who are also called Torguts and belong to one of the four tribes of Oirat. The Torguts that repaired to Russia in 1618 returned to China in 1771, in the days of the Emperor CH'IEN LUNG, and experienced fantastic adventures on the way. Quite a large part of the tribe remained domiciled on the western shores of the lower course of the Volga, however, and their capital, Elista, has recently been much spoken of. In 1921, after KOLCHAK's collapse and after ANNENKOV crossing the boundaries of Sinkiang, part of this tribe retired to Qara-shahr, and at the time of our stay in Urumchi and Qara-shahr these few Kalmuks were under the protection of the Torgut prince SENGTSEN GEGEN KHAN. Thanks to his friendship with that prince, who was murdered in a dastardly manner a few years later by Governor General CHIN SHU-JEN, HASLUND also managed to gain the confidence of the Qara-shahr Torguts, the former Volga Kalmuks, and was at liberty to record their songs on his little Edison. The book contains a number of songs also from the Buriat Soviet Republic in eastern Siberia. The bulk of the material, however, is from Outer and Inner Mongolia, the former under Russian and the latter at present partly under Japanese suzerainty. When the remaining melodies and texts recorded by HASLUND-CHRISTENSEN during the expedition have been printed and published, this work will not be complete but nevertheless it must be considered very representative and of great value.

This first volume in the series contains about 90 songs, many of which are claimed by Mongol tradition to date from the period of greatness under CHINGGIS KHAN and which have thus throughout 700 years, century after century, year after year, been sung around the camp fires in the black, grey or white *yurts* of the Mongols, in war and peace, in the pasture-lands of the herds or on the way to new pastures. A couple of the songs were first heard when the first Bogdo Gegen was on his way from Tibet to Urga.

Others are of an epic type and glorify warriors and heroes, their wonderful attributes and exploits. Historically important events have time after time been described in poetry and music. Love was often and readily made the subject of poetical effusions. The sweet melancholy of the young girl on leaving her parental home and her touching parting from the tent-village where she spent her childhood is sung of in tender strains and around the singer the lovers gather and listen with zest. The majestic nature of this boundless land of grass, its fascinating beauty and unfathomable mysticism is sung of in numerous Mongol hymns of indescribable charm. Didactic and moral poems alternate with flowers of lyric poetry, all carried by the wings of music from generation to generation. Mysterious and incomprehensible, they have sounded in the ears of the Mongol children and again and again they have returned on the solemn occasions of life while the sun has set in blood and the moon, as mysterious as the song, has shed its silver over the tents in the stillness of the night. The boundless greatness of the desert is probably still a mystery to the nomads. The only thing the old Mongols know for certain is that their love for the steppe and the desert has ever grown stronger in their souls.

Our experiences in and the memories we retain from our years in Mongolia and the Gobi are almost always intimately connected with singing and music. On our long journey from Pao-t'ou through Inner Mongolia and offshoots from the Gobi our three hundred camels were tended and driven by twenty splendid and powerful Mongols wearing the becoming dress of their country and, like ourselves, riding two-humped Bactrian camels. If I was then riding in the middle of the caravan, I would almost for certain hear singing before or behind me. If we were making our way through or between the dunes a scarcely audible rustle was heard, created by the pads of the camels sweeping through the dry sand, a contribution to the melodies breaking the stillness and enhancing the mystery of the desert.

When we left the steppes and the sparsely scattered nomadic camps and steered our course out across the desolate sea of the desert, the singing of our Mongols assumed a more melancholy and elegiac note as if the tune and words were intended to express their longing for the wealth of the steppes and for their families in the tent-villages at home. But their songs also conveyed what sounded like an echo of the greatness of the desert and of the magnificent and imposing scenery that surrounded them, which they had known and loved since their tender years. Boundless is the desert, it extends in all directions to the very edge of the horizon. In spite of its poverty, solitude and silence it possesses the same fascination as the sea and one can never grow tired of it. It affords the soul rest and repose to know that also tomorrow, in weeks and months to come the same scenery will unfold its uniform desolation before us. In this fabulous milieu there is no more suitable music than that of the Mongols. This is quite natural, for the songs sung by them throughout the centuries are impressed with the stamp of the unique and overpowering East-Asiatic scenery.

Finally, however, we reached the desert river Edsen-gol, where the autumn wind moaned in the tops of the poplars and the leaves were already tinged with yellow and red.

An episode from those days remains vivid in my memory. It was in the middle of October, 1927. The headquarters of the caravan were on the bank of the Edsen-gol, whence the various sections of the expedition made their separate journeys of discovery. HENNING HASLUND-CHRISTENSEN and I had seated ourselves in a boat, which our people had made out of two poplar trunks, and had drifted down the branch of the river which under the name of the Dunda-gol falls out into the salt-lake Sogho-nor. In a deep narrow channel the dark clear water of the river flows through the forest, the trunks of the trees resembling the peristyle of a fairy-palace, their crowns in wondrous autumn tints blending into a vault over this enchanting path. In an idyllic park-like part on the left bank stood LARSON, the Swedish Mongol chief, and one of our Mongols, BANCHE, who had gone riding down the bank. They suggested that we spend the night in that wonderful neighbourhood. We jumped ashore, arranged our simple camp and made an agreeably crackling fire in the cool evening.

The sun set, the twilight spread its shadows over the ground, it grew ever darker and the flames lit up the nearby trunks while those farther off appeared as ghosts in the dark.

Then BANCHE picked up his flute and began to play, to begin with slowly, softly and dreamily. But soon his tune grew more vivid and living and it was noticeable that inadvertently he put the magic scenery surrounding him into music. The murmur of the water round a trunk that had got stuck in the river-bottom, the plashing round the feet of the camels when they found a shallow place and went out into the water, the rustling of the evening breeze in the tree-tops — all these sounds were recorded by the flute. BANCHE's playing seemed to fill the whole of this majestic hall: the nature, the air, all vibrated with it; we and our camels were carried away by this irresistible atmosphere; the trees in their yellow autumn garb seemed to listen, and even the flames of the camp-fire seemed to dance like the cobra when the fakir plays his flute.

After a while BANCHE lowered the flute and began to sing. His song was extempore and dictated by the feeling of the moment. He sang of our longing for the river during our long months in the desert. He described our coming to the forests of the Edsen-gol and compared it to the arrival at a long looked-forward-to goal. In his simple words we heard the softly purling water along the banks of the Dunda-gol, the sough of the wind in the crowns of the poplars, and we saw a sparkling star or two where the leaves had thinned out and fallen to the ground to form a carpet as yellow as in the temple of a Lama monastery or to tread a last dance before the advent of winter.

Thus BANCHE sang the whole evening and far into the night, now and again interrupting his singing to play the flute. Certainly it is the surroundings, their beauty and atmosphere, that inspire the singer and fire his imagination. A music hall such as the forest on the Dunda-gol is ideal, but also the *yurt* on the steppe at home, where his friends listen with rapt attention around the fire, fosters the inspiration of the Mongol, whether he sings, blows the flute, or lets the bow run across the strings of the fiddle. In the *yurt,* on the steppe, in the desert or in the wood, Mongol music is at its best. In our ears it may sound exotic to begin with. But when you have familiarized yourself with the life and ways of the Mongols, you soon learn to love their songs and the melancholy tunes they bring forth from their simple instruments.

These tunes are a dying echo from times of greatness and of fantastic achievements in the history of Asia. They vibrate with pride over a world-embracing past and with melancholy that the survivors of this people have lost their power and their importance and are doomed to oppression by mighty neighbours.

The dreamy rhythm of the elegiac and erotic songs is still heard in the land of the Mongols and it is gratifying that a young Danish traveller, who has spent many years of his life with that genial people, thanks to his ear and energy has been able to collect and record the tunes and words while it is still time.

This book thus throws open a foreign world of tunes to those interested in music. The Mongol songs will not die out but will still exist even in the future when they may no longer be heard on the steppes and when there is no longer anyone to sing of the woods on the banks of the Dunda-gol.

Sven Hedin.

ON THE TRAIL OF ANCIENT MONGOL TUNES

BY

HENNING HASLUND-CHRISTENSEN

As far back as we can see in the history of Mongolia we find it inhabited by nomads, who at shorter or longer intervals started migrations that frequently took the form of great crusades of conquest against the surrounding kingdoms.

ATTILA and his fierce Huns, who swept Europe in the fifth century, as well as many of the hordes that followed in his footsteps, came from Mongolia; and "The Great Wall of China" was a gigantic attempt to check the constant stream of hardened steppe-folk who were perpetually plundering "The Middle Kingdom".

The last nomad conquerors in the grand style were the Mongols, and the man who rallied and inspired the Central Asiatic tribes to the greatest feats of arms was the famous CHINGGIS KHAN (1162—1227), of whom HARALD LAMB so aptly writes: "A Mongol nomad who had never seen a city founded an empire that ruled half the world; a hunter and a herder of beasts outmanoeuvred and crushed all the armies of three civilizations; a barbarian who did not know the use of writing made a code of laws for fifty peoples."

CHINGGIS KHAN made himself the absolute master of all the country between Armenia and Korea, from Tibet to the Volga; and at his death the power of the Mongols was so firmly established that no attempt was made to prevent his sons from taking over the reins of power in the occupied kingdoms.

Some ten years after the death of CHINGGIS KHAN "The Golden Horde" rode westward under BATU's leadership. On their way they stormed Kiev and subjugated all the tribes on the Volga.

The German barons with their king and their whole clergy rallied round the cross in a holy war against the dreaded Mongols; but everywhere the yak-tail standards of the latter were victorious, and when they finally retired it was due to the sudden death of the great Khan in distant Kara Korum.

The power of the Mongols culminated under CHINGGIS KHAN's grandson, KHUBLAI (1215—94), who added Tibet to the conquests of his ancestors and founded the Mongol Yuan dynasty in China (1260—1368). — It was KHUBLAI who transferred his residence and the Mongol headquarters from Kara Korum in the heart of Mongolia to Kanbalu (Peking) in China, which was undoubtedly opposed to his great ancestor's admonition to acquire the accomplishments of the enemy without allowing oneself to be tempted by the way of life that had given rise to his weaknesses.

Nor was it long before the Mongol leaders in Kanbalu as well as the small and scattered Mongol garrisons in China began to show the symptoms of degeneration that barbarian conquerors so easily acquire when they expose themselves to the peaceful and leisurely life of an old civilization. They lost, too, the military superiority that was indispensable if they were to continue to dominate the subject peoples by whom they were so vastly outnumbered.

When in 1368 the Mongols were driven out of China they had to fly right up to northern Mongolia, and the Chinese Ming dynasty that had taken over the power in China was for a long time able to defend "The Great Wall" against all attacks by the steppe-folk.

At the same time as the unifying central Mongol leadership fell into decay, the power in the other parts of the empire began to decline. As new generations of Mongols, through inter-marriage and other influences, acquired the culture and religion of the occupied countries, the strength arising from their former solidarity was succeeded by disintegrating intrigues that at times resulted in violent strife among themselves. The inevitable outcome was the decay of the empire. Numbers of Mongol descendants were in time completely absorbed by the populations that their forefathers had ruled; others, however, managed to preserve their original faith and way of life in small isolated feudal communities, remote from the mother country to which they owed their origin.

The Mongols' rôle as makers of world-history has long since been ended; but in Siberia, Afghanistan, Russia, Manchuria and all the intermediate regions it is still possible to trace descendants of the proud hordes that once conquered, united and ruled the greatest empire in the world.

Baber, the last Mongol ruler in the Jagatai Khanate, still retained, after in 1500 being driven from Central Asia, so much of his forefathers' virility that he was able to lead a new crusade of conquest, resulting in the dominion of the Great Moguls in India (1526—1857); but he had already exchanged the old yak-tail standard of the Mongols for the green banner of the prophet.

The fate of the Chinese Ming dynasty, however, proved no exception to that of all earlier dynasties — it, too, in time lost the strength that had brought it to power; and as the Chinese became weaker, new and hardened generations of nomads, descendants of the Mongols who in 1368 had been driven from China, began to draw back from the much poorer country of northern Mongolia to the more enticing South. By the end of the 16th century they had occupied the whole of what is now South Mongolia, where they settled in independent groups. These often called themselves by new names, and we find only few of the clan-names that had achieved fame in the former periods of greatness.

As a general rule, the culture of a people changes more rapidly than its racial characteristics. The professor of anatomy at Peking Union Medical College, Dr Paul Stevenson, was of the opinion that merely by using the methods of physical anthropology one could determine the mutual relationships of the present tribes and folk-groups in Central Asia and their descent from the famous hordes that in the periods of nomad-greatness made world-history, if one could collect among them a sufficiently large and comprehensive anthropometric material.

It seemed to be a matter of the greatest importance to attain clearness in these questions, and on becoming a member of the Sven Hedin expedition in 1927 I gladly undertook the task of carrying out anthropometric measurements on the native population in the regions through which the expedition was to travel.

But the more I had to do with the established method of work the less I believed in the possibility of achieving satisfactory results in this way.

Time and again it happened that in the region I was investigating I found a certain age-group of the population showing racial characteristics that differed anthropometrically from those of other individuals in the tribe. On several such occasions I was able to constate that in the birth-year of the age-group in question the tribe had been exposed to miscegenation. The more isolated such a tribe lived, the more distinctly could one trace anthropometrically the consequences of the passage of a Chinese robber-band, of an invasion by Siberian Cossacks or a clash with Mohammedan insurgents.

The strangers had all hastened farther on their journey towards other regions and fresh adventures, without leaving other traces of their passage than the strain of foreign blood that flowed in the veins of the offspring they sowed on their way.

These children, who had never known their real fathers, had been conceived at the tent-hearths that were fed and watched by their Mongolian mothers; they had been nurtured with the songs and legends that had resounded at the tent-hearths of the tribe for many generations; they had taken part in the same games and sports as the other children; and they had been trained to the occupations, the morals and the view of life that constituted the characteristic cultural inheritance of the tribe from a remote past. To all appearances they were genuine and fully accredited members of the tribe, but they were a living proof that the anthropometric characteristics of a tribe can be changed in the course of a single night.

How many similar and still more radical changes must the various folk-groups not have undergone in a country like Mongolia, whose male population so often went off to ravage other tracts while their women stayed at home with the children and old men to keep the eternal hearth-fires of the tribe alight?

It thus became clear to me that the way to the goal in view must follow a more stable and intimate line than that given by the anthropometric pointers upon which we had hitherto relied. One must look back over the past in the light of the tent-hearths, for their sacred flames are the centre of both the family and the tribal life; it is here that the traditions live, and it is around the hearth that the ancient words and airs containing the oldest and most intimate characteristics of the tribe are confided from generation to generation to bridge the gulf from past to present.[1]

Having reached this conviction, I could with a clear conscience go on to a new field of work, that I knew would be a source of much pleasure to me, for the legends and folk-songs of Mongolia, with their incomparable flavour of romance and their splendid fantasy, have always been very dear to me.

During the last few decades Mongolia has been explored by a number of expeditions, whose results throw light upon the geographical, geologic, archæological and other conditions of the country. The experiences of some of these travellers have been published in scientific or popular form; but neither the printed word nor pictures can reproduce that which more than anything else reflects the soul of the country and the most intimate cultural inheritance of the nomad tribes that are gradually dying out. One must become attuned to the proud and melancholy tones of the Mongol melodies in order rightly to feel the magnificent and impressive beauty of the mighty deserts and steppes; one must listen to the words in the old folk-songs to realize that these isolated and frugal herdsmen are descendants of the men who seven centuries ago were the most powerful people in the world. — The power and magnificence of their period of greatness has long since vanished, but the memory of the past has been confided from father to son generation after generation, right up to the threshold of our own culture-levelling times.

The interest in Mongol music is not new, and the oldest written scores that I have been able to trace are four little melodies that Joh. Georg Gmelin, a member of the famous Vitus Bering expedition, published in 1742. The melodies were taken down in the Siberian town of Krasnoyarsk in 1740, and derive from four Buriat tribes who even at that early date were of mixed blood with Russian peasants and Cossacks.

In 1850 the English missionary's son J. S. Stallybrass noted down some Buriat melodies that he had learned as a lad in the Siberian town of Selinginsk. — It is of great interest to compare these Buriat melodies that were noted down so long ago with the songs that are still current in Mongolia; but in judging them it should be borne in mind that Stallybrass was only a lad of fifteen when he left the English mission station in Siberia, and that he wrote down the melodies from memory nine years after his arrival in England.

[1] The number of anthropometric measurements that I took on my journeys amounts to 170, covering a great part of Central Asia from Manchuria in the east to Tibet and Turkistan in the west. The time that I spent on this work, however, was not wasted, for it gives a picture of the racial characteristics of the various folk-groups to-day that may serve as interesting comparative material for similar investigations in the future.

A part of the material is being worked up at present by Dr Paul Stevenson, and some of it has been of use in other respects.

In 1915 the Belgian priest P. JOSEPH VAN OOST of the Scheut Mission published a valuable treatise on the music of the Ordos Mongols, in which were included a number of musical scores.[2] In the summer of 1925 I often had the pleasure of being entertained by Father VAN OOST in the old Mongolian frontier town of Kuku Khoto, where he had sought refuge after a long and self-sacrificing life in the sterile desert of the Ordos Mongols. Most often I would find him sitting at the piano, while his old fingers coaxed forth strange, melancholy melodies from the ancient instrument. They were tones that found an immediate response in me, but is was not until I had myself become familiar with the country to which the old priest so often returned in his dreams, that I really learned to understand their precious meaning and their full beauty.

In addition, a number of Russian writers have occupied themselves with Mongol music, but except for RUDNEV, who in 1909 published a work on the Mongol songs thitherto known,[3] the specimens that I have found available have been treated by writers of the new Russia, whose political views seem to have led them to look perhaps too exclusively forward instead of back into the past.

When in 1929 I had my first leave of absence after more than six years uninterrupted stay in Asia, I was met in the little frontier town of Chuguchaq by Princess NIRGIDMA of the Torgut tribe. The princess came direct from Europe, in whose cities she had spent the same number of years as I had passed in travelling about the steppes of her native country. She had much to relate of the Occident, and I on my side told her of the rich impressions I had taken away from her people. Before we parted we had agreed upon an intimate collaboration for the realization of my plans; but fate willed, as it turned out, that seven whole years should pass before our paths crossed again. When we saw each other again in Peking, in 1936, she had been driven from her native soil by the Soviet; but before her flight she had managed to take down 18 of her tribe's folk-songs, that were published in Paris in 1937.[4]

My own work on the Mongolian folk-songs was begun in the autumn of 1928 on a journey to the grazing-grounds of the Qara-shahr Torguts in Eastern Turkistan.[5]

The Torguts at Qara-shahr are descendants of the few survivors of the Torgut horde from the historical flight from the River Volga in the South of Russia, that they left in 1771 to seek their way back to the grasslands that their forefathers had left in 1618.

[2] OOST, P. JOSEPH VAN: La musique chez les Mongols des Urdus, Anthropos, May-Aug. 1915—16. Vols. X—XI; 3, 4.

[3] RUDNEV, A. D.: Melodii mongolskikh plemen, in Zap. Imp. Russkago Geogr. Obsč. po. otd. Etn. t. XXXIV.

[4] La Princesse NIRGIDMA DE TORHOUT et Mdm. HUMBERT-SAUVAGEOT: Dix-huit Chants et Poèmes Mongols. Paris, Geuthner 1937.

[5] About the Qara-shahr Torguts and their history see: Men and Gods in Mongolia, London 1935.

I could scarcely have sought out a locality more encouraging for my work than the Torguts' grazing-grounds in the Yulduz Mountains; and a number of happy circumstances led SENGTSEN GEGEN, the Torgut ruler and the last in the succession of Mongolian Great Khans (he was murdered in 1932 by the Chinese), to meet my plans with understanding interest and helpfulness. I was thus able to get the Torgut Khan to assemble the best singers in the vast region over which he ruled; and since among these were members of a good many of the Mongol tribes living in Eastern Turkistan, I was able in the course of the winter to take records of a representative collection of West Mongolian songs and melodies.

A number of these, as well as some of the song-texts I had noted, were unhappily lost in an avalanche in the Himalayas, but 54 phonograph cylinders were saved, and constitute what I have called Collection I. On the subjoined map the regions that are represented in Collection I are marked with double hatching.[6]

During my visit in Stockholm in 1929 I had the opportunity to play the wax-cylinders I had brought home to an audience of musical experts, and the interest they aroused confirmed me in my opinion that besides for Asiatic scholars they might also be of interest for students of music. When in September of the same year I returned to Mongolia I took with me a new Edison phonograph and a large number of wax cylinders. Illness arising out of an accident, however, soon drove me back to Europe; but another member of the expedition Dr G. MONTELL, took the phonograph with him on a journey to the Edsen-gol, where he was able to record a number of Torgut songs that constitute an interesting supplement to the songs noted down by Princess NIRGIDMA and to my Collection I.

It took several years before I had sufficiently recovered from the effects of the avalanche accident that had interrupted my work in 1930 to be able to think of a new expedition to Asia; but by the spring of 1936 I was once more ready to start. The field-work of the SVEN HEDIN expedition, however, had been wound up one year previously, and this time I undertook the journey on behalf of the Danish National Museum.

As the point of departure for the new expedition I chose Hsinking, the hyper-modern capital of Manchukuo, that the Japanese had in an astonishingly short time conjured up on the steppe that only a few years before had belonged to the domain of the Gorlos, the easternmost of all the Mongol tribes. From Hsinking the expedition was to work its way to the north-west, to try and make contact with Golds and other North Manchurian and Siberian tribes, that were already represented in the Danish National Museum, and with the Buriats and North Mongols whose folk-music was to some extent known through the work of the writers mentioned in the foregoing. When this contact had been established it was my intention

[6] The notes of some of the melodies comprising Collection I have been printed in "Tents in Mongolia", London 1933 and in "Men and Gods in Mongolia", London 1935.

to push on to the south-west, through regions whose music and ethnography were as yet unexplored, to the north of Ordos, where Father VAN OOST had already achieved so much, and farther west to get in touch with the West Mongolian tribes whose melodies I had recorded in 1928/29.

Before my departure I had conferred with interested musical experts in Europe, and we had agreed that if the material I brought back was to be of any real use to musical scholarship here at home it was important that it should be as technically perfect as possible. I therefore paid a visit to Dr ANDERS DYMLING, the then head of the Swedish Broadcasting Corporation, and I could not have addressed myself to anyone with more understanding for my work. Dr DYMLING at once entered into my plans with enthusiasm, and before long he had the technical department of the Broadcasting Corporation at work on the construction of a recording apparatus that would meet my special requirements. It must be an instrument that could be used in the desert, where no electric power was available; it must be able to stand up to the unavoidably rough transports of an Asiatic journey; the many different parts of the equipment must be composed of equally heavy units, that were adapted to the carrying capacity of a camel; and the whole apparatus must be so simply constructed that a layman might carry out all conceivable repairs.

The complete instrument consisted of ten parts, besides 300 blank records and the tins of petrol and oil that were necessary for the running of the motor. The apparatus consisted of a petrol motor that drove a generator that charged two accumulators of aeroplane type. These accumulators drove a converter that converted the battery tension of 24 volts to a 220 volt 50 cycles alternating current, and this was connected to the recording apparatus. The latter was provided with an amplifier and a recording unit with a synchronized motor and cutting head and pick-up. The record motor (of syncron type) was driven with the alternating current from the converter, and its speed could be kept constant with the help of a regulating resistance. As microphone I used a common carbon microphone for broadcasting, that was connected to a battery in the recording cabinet by means of a 100-meter cable.

It was not without considerable trepidation that I set off with this complicated machinery; but in spite of the difficult transports, sandstorms and cold and other trials to which it was often exposed, it never sustained any damage that I was unable to repair myself, and with its aid I succeeded in taking 124 recordings from tribes whose folk-music had not previously been known.

It is a part of this material, Collection 2, that is presented in this work.

On the subjoined map the regions represented in Collection 2 are marked with numbers from 1 to 91. The numerals correspond to the numbers of the melodies and give the approximate spots from which they derive.

It was on this journey that I realized with terrible clearness that the age-old Mongol nomad-culture was being completely effaced, before science had managed to record even its most important features.

When in 1923 I arrived in Central Asia for the first time I found the whole of this isolated world, with its sparse nomad population, like a living reminder of a remote past. It was as if the life of a begone time had here found a sanctuary that seemed to have given it a lasting existence in complete sequestration, untouched by all the manifold changes and the noisy development of the surrounding world. On sober reflection I was often struck by the strange thought that the life I found here was in all essentials the same as the life that Friar Odoric, Marco Polo and other classical writers on Asia had found and described more than six centuries ago. But in time one came to realize that life was lived here in such intimate agreement with the inexplicable atmosphere of eternity that invested these vast landscapes, that the population had long since achieved a philosophy and a mode of life that were so harmoniously right that they were inviolate.

I learned that in the nomads' world the hurrying hand of the clock had come to a standstill. Time was reckoned by sunrises and full-moons; and the changes of the sun and moon are not so rapid that one does not have time to think one's thoughts to an end and digest the impressions given by each new day.

The Mongolian nomads are a people of herdsmen and hunters, who with their light tents wander all their lives between the watering-places that are the necessary condition of their life and that of their cattle-herds. The home of the Mongol nomad is wherever the wanderings of his herd of cattle take him. He does not count any spot on earth as his own, for everything is the property of the gods. But where there is free pasture he enjoys the privileged usufruct of the nomad, and everything by which his tent is framed: the steppe, the sky, and the mountain-horizon is *his* — just as much as the water that the watering-place gives him. This generous elementary rule of the nomads' country makes itself felt as a greeting of welcome that meets one everywhere, and that in some strange way disarms the homesickness of the traveller from the west.

The Mongols of the old stock have an intense aversion to houses, for the free steppe must not be bound by heavy masonry. For the monasteries, however, this rule does not apply, for they are the abode of the gods; and the only fixed buildings in Mongolia were until quite recently the scattered temples in which lived the Buddhist monks.

The Mongol nomad is in the eyes of the Chinese a barbarian of low standing, who lives an uncomfortable life on account of his stupidity and devotes himself to such primitive pleasures as hunting and wild rides over an uncultivated landscape. The Mongol, for his part, pities the Chinese, who is tied down to house and fields; and he feels the deepest contempt for men who prefer the gentle donkey as a mount to the newly captured steppe-horse. The true nomad denies with all the fervour of conviction that his culture is more primitive than that of city-dwellers and peasants, whom he regards as earth-bound slaves, excluded from the glorious adventure of a strongly pulsating natural life.

The reason why a feeling of affinity arises so much more naturally between a European and a Mongol than between a Mongol and a Chinese is doubtless to be sought in the fact that the Chinese, with his ancient and refined civilization, has become farther removed from the simple springs of life than the European. For the Chinese, form has become more important than natural instinct, and the copy is more admired than the original. He will admire the subtle colour-scheme in a piece of artistic embroidery and the elegance and delicacy of line in a landscape painting, and remain impassive and untouched by the living beauty of an actual landscape. The Chinese lacks the Mongol's spontaneous ability to feel Nature's distinct and various shades strongly and immediately, to extract from them a healthy joy of life and fresh creative impulses.

We are inclined to dismiss the Mongol nomads as ignorant and superstitious people; but one cannot live with them without rejoicing at their aspirations to beauty, that are guided by a fine spiritual instinct. They can boast a dignified etiquette, a deeply rooted social order, a real feeling for ethical and aesthetic values, and their spiritual eye follows the large lines of the powers of Nature.

An understanding study of the nomads' special gift would undoubtedly be a source of healthy renewal for the nervous life of this over-industrialized and intellectualized world.

A Chinese legend relates that the Emperor FU HSI was the Father of Music. FU HSI, who lived 3 000 years before the beginning of the Christian calendar, is also credited with having taught men to hunt, to break in horses, to keep cattle and to make fire. It is worthy of note that in this ancient Chinese legend the man who taught his fellows these nomad occupations was also supposed to be the world's first musician.

The conquest of China by the Mongols brought in its train new and strong currents for the stagnant pond in which Chinese culture had sunk. CHINGGIS KHAN and his Mongol horsemen had already introduced Mongol songs into China, that later left traces in the Chinese verse-forms. A large number of the classical dramas that are still performed in the Chinese theatres were written under the Mongol Yuan dynasty; and under the same dynasty Chinese painting was enriched by a completely new epoch with a marked sense for bright and brilliant colours.

It is said that KHUBLAI KHAN introduced into China an altogether new musical scale, so strikingly reminiscent of our major scale that one might think it was borrowed from Europe. But about 1300 A. D., European music was probably confined to the Gregorian song, in which the major scale does not occur; and this seems to indicate that a scale of 8 notes at that early date was the national scale of the Mongols.

On my return to Central Asia in 1936 I found that the few years during which I had been absent in the civilized world had brought about greater and more radical changes than the whole of the previous five hundred years put together.

The contented nomads who had formerly lived their dream-like existence in undisturbed isolation had suddenly become a focus of interest for the outside world. Mongolia, that had hitherto been a poor and ignored country, had become strategically important, and two rival powers had each occupied a half of the nomad lands. Neither of the powers in question wished to be observed by outsiders. Foreigners had been forbidden to enter northern Mongolia as early as 1926, and the restrictions against foreigners staying in South and East Mongolia were continually being made more stringent.

The occupying powers had begun to enrol Mongol youth in their respective schools and armies, and the whole population was now being exposed to the effective batteries of modern propagandistic technique.

It was with a feeling of inexpressible sadness that I was now obliged to seek out the representatives of the older time in isolated hiding-places. Chieftains who had formerly guided the destinies of proud tribes were now losing their authority over the youth of their own clan; troubadours who had themselves spent their youth at the feet of the old masters to learn the chants and folk-songs of the past were now without a single disciple to whom they could pass on their precious inheritance; and story-tellers who had once been honoured guests in every camp had now to yield the place of honour at the hearth-fire to the young men who could bring news from one of the propaganda-centres of the great powers.

I found myself face to face with the inescapable thought that all the ancient lore that these feeble old men would take with them when they went to their fathers would, if it were not now saved, be finally and irrevocably lost to the world. None of the old folk-songs existed in writing; like so much of the old lore, they had been passed on from generation to generation in the families that for centuries had administered the precious cultural inheritance of the people. Certainly, there does exist in Mongolia a form for the writing of musical scores, but as this is used only in connection with the clerical music introduced from Tibet, the already rusting key to an understanding of the most intimate and delicate chords in the nomad soul would disappear with the last of the old troubadours.

For myself, Mongol music and the moods that are evoked by the old folk-songs are a great personal pleasure, by which I have often been entranced, and which has always been able to banish the feeling of emptiness that a European may experience during a prolonged stay among a foreign people in a remote country. These songs have helped me to an understanding of the aesthetic values in the often bleak landscapes of their origin. It was the singing milk-maids and the melancholy tones of the caravan-folk in the dead stillness of the desert that gave me an insight into the deepest thoughts of the people, and on the evenings when I have sat at the warming tent-fire while the soughing wind from the steppe evoked the very atmosphere of what had been sung, it was the songs and epics of the old men that helped me to glimpse the contours of the mighty pictures that make up the great and richly changing history of the nomads.

The great American expeditions under the leadership of ROY CHAPMAN ANDREWS had returned home in 1930 without ANDREWS having been able to obtain a renewed permit to enter any part of Mongolia. And SVEN HEDIN's "Wandering University" had also wound up its field-work in 1933, while its numerous members were now dispersed in their respective home-countries to immerse themselves in the work of classifying and arranging the results of their labours. In the years 1936—37 the members of my Danish expedition were the only representatives of Occidental research in Mongolia, and there was no indication of new expeditions setting out as long as conditions were as they were.

Accordingly, in the spring of 1937 I resolved to return home in order to submit my new plans to those in my home-land who might be interested, hoping to procure the necessary capital and new expedition-members for the realization of these plans.

During the months I was away in Europe, my two collaborators were to go on with several of the tasks we had already begun, and prepare for the arrival of the new members. Before setting out on my journey home, however, I had assured myself of a permit for the new expedition to enter the country from the authorities who were in power in that part of Mongolia.

In Denmark my plans for an extended expedition were at once met with great interest, and with a full understanding of the haste that was called for by the situation the Danish Government, in concert with the Carlsberg Fund, quickly placed at my disposal the required funds. At the same time the desired members were assured for the expedition.

The sound-recordings I brought home with me from Manchuria and eastern Mongolia proved to be of such quality and interest that I was given the opportunity of broadcasting a number of them from several of the European broadcasting stations. This brought me into touch with fresh circles of musical experts who were interested in Mongolian folk-music, and before my departure I left the recordings comprising Collection 2 with Dr SVEN HEDIN, who entrusted the difficult task of writing down the material according to our system of notation to Dr E. EMSHEIMER, an ethnographer with musical experience now domiciled in Stockholm.

In order to facilitate Dr EMSHEIMER's treatment of Collection 2, the data connected with the material that I had amassed on my journeys was also placed at his disposal.

The new expedition, that was sent out by The Royal Danish Geographical Society, included in its equipment a new and improved recording apparatus, that had also been constructed and placed at my disposal by the Swedish Broadcasting Corporation.

When in September 1939 this expedition had to interrupt its work in Asia owing to the outbreak of the new world-war, we had recorded with this apparatus 167 new folk-songs among the tribes living in the regions marked on the map with arrow-heads; and it is this material that we refer to as Collection 3. It is my hope that we may be able to commence the work of classifying and arranging Collection 3 by the time the present paper is published, and that it may see the light in the comparatively near future.

That the Collections 2 and 3 have been arranged and published before Collection 1 is explained by the impossibility under present conditions of procuring materials for the requisite number of copies of the original wax cylinders.

I cannot regard my work of collecting Mongol folk-music as concluded, and it is my hope that I or others may later be in a position to carry on this work until all the tones from a remote and great past that may still linger on in remote corners of Mongolia have been recorded and made available to science. But if this may not be, I am happy to be able to state that the material that has already been collected is so comprehensive, both as regards quantity and localities, that it may be said to represent the world of the Mongol nomads in its entire extent. — It is a material that will preserve for a late posterity a wealth of echoes from a music that for the greatest nomad people in the world meant the very core of harmony between earth and sky and man.

As may be seen from the map, the material in the three collections covers the ground from the Gorlos tribe in Manchuria to the Torguts in remote Eastern Turkistan, and from the Buriats in Siberia to the Chakhar tribe, now dying out, at the edge of "The Great Wall of China". Further additions to the material will probably only be new variations of what is already known through the three existing collections.

It is as yet too early to broach the question as to the degree in which the musical material so far collected may help in the determination of the mutual relationships of the many tribes and folk-groups living in the Central Asia of our day, and the descent of these peoples from the famous hordes that once made world-history. A number of specimens taken at random can only serve to strengthen my hope that interesting results in this respect may be attained when the material as a whole has been collated and finally arranged.

As is shown in the map, Collection 2 includes the Buriat, Chipchin, Daghur, Ölet, Jalait, Khorchin, Khorchin-Jasaktu, Gorlos, Tumet, Barin, Kharchin and Chakhar tribes.

On the journey on which this collection was made I began work in Wang-yin Sume ("The King's Monastery"), that is the old seat of the chieftain of the Jasaktu *banner* of the Khorchin tribe.

Even in the time of the Ming dynasty Chakhar was the name of a part of the steppe-land that stretched away immediately outside "The Great Wall"; and it was here that the chieftain who had inherited the Mongolian ruling title settled with his family and his followers, who afterwards took the name of the occupied country as the name of their tribe. LIKDAN KHAN (1592—1634), who belonged to this ruling family (he was a direct descendant of CHINGGIS KHAN through twenty-one generations), laid claim to his rightful power as the Chief Khan of all the Mongols; and he succeeded in bringing a number of the surrounding tribes under his control. He would probably have succeeded in uniting all Mongols under his standard and reconquering China from the enfeebled Ming dynasty, if a new power had not raised its head. This new factor was the Manchus who were descended from the Nu-chen (Jurchit) Tartars, who had ruled the whole of North China for more than a hundred years, till in 1233 they were overthrown by the Mongols.

In order to escape LIKDAN's suzerainty the East Mongolian chieftains turned to the Manchus for aid, and a Mongolian-Manchu army advanced against the Chakhar tribe, that was beaten in 1633. LIKDAN himself perished on his flight westward in 1634.

At the end of the 17th century the Chakhar tribe tried to win back their lost independence, which resulted in the extirpation of the ruling family of the tribe by the Manchus and its reorganization according to the Manchurian military-*banner* system. In the following decades Chakhar's eight *banners* did excellent service as a part of the Manchurian cavalry, in which capacity they were sent to Kansu, Altai and Ili, where one may still find their descendants.

After the fall of the Manchu dynasty in 1912 the Chinese colonization of Chakhar commenced; and to-day about 80 % of their steppe has been transformed to Chinese fields. A small remainder of the tribe is now crowded together in the northernmost part of the vast steppes that they once ruled, where they eke out a shabby and impoverished existence. The last traces of their original culture are rapidly disappearing.

The Khorchin tribe to-day is a confederation of six *banners,* whose chiefs are all said to be direct descendants of the celebrated KHABTU KHASAR, CHINGGIS KHAN's eldest brother, who in 1214 led the left wing of the Mongolian army in the attack on China.

The Khorchin Mongols still relate numberless legends in praise of KHABTU KHASAR's enormous strength and skill as an archer, and his fame is sung in several of the old folk-songs (see song No. 55).

Until 1425, when the West Mongols drove the Khorchin tribe to what is now Manchuria, they had their grazing grounds in northern Mongolia. In Manchuria their relations with the tribes of that country were alternately hostile and peaceful, and in 1626 they were among the first Mongol tribes to join the then emerging Manchus. In 1644 they were allies of the Manchus in the latter's storming of Peking, that led to the fall of the Ming dynasty and the ascent of China's Dragon Throne by the Manchus.

K'ANG HSI (1662—1723), the most outstanding ruler of the Manchu dynasty and one of the greatest emperors who ever ruled "The Middle Kingdom", was in intimate relations with the governing family of the Khorchin tribe, for both his intelligent and highly esteemed mother and his beloved empress had been born Khorchin princesses, and many of the tribe's "White Boned"[7] descendants took Manchu princesses in marriage.

In this connection it is worth noting that K'ANG HSI, in whose veins there thus flowed more Mongol than Manchurian blood, tried in vain to bring Chinese music back to the older and more beautiful form, that it had obtained in the time of the Yuan dynasty.

These many ties of blood with the most powerful dynasty of the period gave the Khorchin tribe both power, influence, wealth and fresh culture, but since all these good things were only reflections of the brilliance at the Imperial Court in Peking, as this waned they too declined.

In the years 1911 to 1913, when the whole of Eastern and South Mongolia was in a state of revolt on account of the Mongols' unswerving loyalty to the fallen Manchu dynasty, the Khorchin tribe was very active, and OTAI, the chief of the Jasaktu *banner,* was one of the foremost leaders of the movement.

The Jasaktu *banner* has its name from the chieftain's hereditary title of honour, which means "sovereign Prince".

The Chinese Republic, that succeeded the Manchu dynasty, put down the revolt with great cruelty. The élite of the tribe's warriors perished in the fight against the terrific odds with which they were faced; many women and children were murdered, their herds of cattle, sheep and horses were taken away, and the rest of their wealth either spoiled or stolen.

When the railway eventually reached the once so virgin steppes of the Khorchin Mongols the Chinese colonization got under way, and by 1930 more than half of the original grazing grounds of the tribe had been converted to Chinese fields.

When the Japanese undertook the conquest of Manchuria in 1931 a fair part of the Mongol youth helped them in the fight against the hereditary enemy — the Chinese. On my arrival at Wang-yin Sume in 1936 the Khorchin Mongols and the other East Mongols in the Hsingan area had attained the status of an autonomous state under Japanese control and authority. There were many signs indicating that the East Mongols were now marching towards a brighter future, for one of the Japanese interests in Mongolia was to re-create wealthy nomad communities that could deliver wool, hides and other raw materials of which the industry of the home-country stood in such pressing need.

The ideals that had now been adopted by the formerly so dispirited Mongol youth had, however, their roots outside the frontiers of their country, and had nothing in common with the traditions of their fathers. It was the generation growing up to manhood that first began to confide in a brighter future, and in all the newly

[7] Chagan Yasa — white bones, implies in Mongolia the same as "blue blood" with us.

erected administrative buildings the chief posts were held by youths. In the modern schools and barracks one met clean-washed children and youths in correct Japanese uniforms. Everywhere energetic work under purposeful Japanese guidance was the order of the day. A network of telegraph-wires connected the cement-coloured buildings, polished cars glided over the new-laid streets, and straight rows of telegraph-poles extended out over the steppe towards other mushroom-like centres for the dissemination of the new era.

But one saw only few horsemen, and none of the younger town-dwellers was clad in the colourful garments of the old days.

At a distance of a kilometer from this mushroom-town were the dominating heights upon which in time past Khorchin chieftains had caused to be erected the beautiful buildings whose name the new community had adopted.

In order to reach the old "King's Monastery" one had first to make one's way through a labyrinth of Chinese bazaar-alleys from whose booths and stands black-clad Chinese shopkeepers offered cheap wares for sale to the stream of poor Chinese peasants passing by. The elaborately carved and decorated shop-signs still announced that these same booths had once sold gold brocades, brightly coloured stuffs, ornamented saddles and such-like splendours to rich and beauty-loving nomads.

While I was questioning a couple of old, white-bearded shopkeepers as to where the original nomad population of the neighbourhood had betaken themselves, I suddenly heard the quavering tones of a conch-horn from the old "King's Monastery", — soft, calling tones that conjured up a mood of expectation and summoned me away from the Japanese model town and the empty noise of the bazaar-alleys to the slender pagodas and the curving silhouettes of roofs that crowned the grassy heights on the horizon.

But the old "King's Monastery", to which the chieftains of an elder time had taken their Manchurian princesses from Peking's Forbidden Imperial City, lay now in crumbling ruins. The gilt roof-tiles of the temples lay like heaps of broken sherds at the foot of the buildings; the straight rows of pillars of the temple-halls stood stripped of their lacquer and gilt ornaments like dead tree-trunks in a scorched forest; and the plinths in the background of the sacred halls, from which gilded gods had once smiled calmly at the worshipping crowds, stood as yawningly empty as the long altar-tables that had once groaned under the weight of rich sacrificial gifts.

All this one time magnificence was now guarded by a little flock of dispirited old men, who crept about like ghosts between the last ragged temple-flags that fluttered in the cold draughts that blew through a thousand cracks and crannies in the dilapidated wall.

In a clammy cell I had a gloomy conversation with the last monks of the monastery. There were still sufficient of them to perform the most necessary rituals, to beat the old drums to keep the powers of darkness at a distance, and to sound the winding conch-horn at sunrise; but their numbers diminished rapidly, and they were sadly anticipating the day when the eternal flame before the last crumbling clay god of the monastery should be extinguished; for in "King's Monastery" there were no young men who would inherit the knowledge and the duties of the past.

After staying for a week with the old monks in "King's Monastery" I knew that with some few exceptions the singers and musicians of the old era had long since fled to remote valleys where they were now endeavouring to spend the rest of their lives in conformity with the traditions of the past.

Upon my asking where these exceptions might be found, who had not fled to remote places of hiding, I finally received the melancholy reply that they were incarcerated in the prison of the town for having been too deeply rooted in the past to be able to understand the message of the new era.

The following morning I went down to the new part of the town, where I demonstrated my wireless set to an admiring crowd of young people. These youths, having satisfied their thirst for technical knowledge, obligingly procured me the desired admission-card to the prison. After spending four days recording the repertoires of the inmates I managed to procure the release of the most interesting of the prisoners, and one fine September morning I set off in company with my minstrel for the remote part of the Khorchin country that had not yet been reached by the new epoch.

SANGRUP, "the All-knowing", had in his youth been the favourite troubadour of Prince OTAI himself, and he knew more of the old songs of his tribe than any of the other singers I met on the whole of this journey. In his young days he had sat at the feet of his deceased master and sung about all those things that gladden a Mongol heart, and his thin fingers could still play in supple accompaniment to the same melancholy songs.

While we journeyed from one grazing-ground to another over the vast plains that he had long given up all hope of seeing again, he talked to me of his own life, of his people and his country; and in the talk and the melodies that he shared with me over the camp-fire in the evenings he vividly recreated fascinating memories, that no other could have revealed to me.

Together with his princely master and the latter's following of grandees from the steppe, he had undertaken the long journey "over the 37 passes"[8] to the glittering and magnificent Peking of the imperial epoch, where in the halls and pavilions of "The Forbidden City" he had entranced proud princes and romantic princesses with his songs and his playing.

He had been rewarded with much favour and rich presents, and when he return-

[8] This was before the Manchurian railways had been laid, and the route between the Khorchin country and Peking was via Jehol, Kalgan and Nankow. The greater part of this route is through mountain-country, and the number of difficult passes to be crossed is 37. This old route is now no more used, but the old Khorchin Mongols remember it well and call it by the number of the passes.

ed to his native steppe he was mounted on a spirited steed, and clad in magnificent brocades and heavy ornaments. No festival was in those times regarded as complete by the Khorchin tribe unless SANGRUP KHURCHI was present, and wherever Mongol tents were pitched he had been in demand as a guest, and always he had been regaled with the best.

During "the black years",[9] like all the other members of his tribe, he lost all his worldly goods, but he had constructed for himself a new stringed instrument, and he still had sufficient voice left to continue consoling and inspiriting the survivors with the mighty songs of the past.

But "the black years" had only been a prelude to the new winds that soon came sweeping in over the old country. The remains of the generation that had fought the last great fight for the freedom of the nomad country soon went to their fathers, with grief and sorrow in their hearts; and the spirit of the new era struck root in the young people, in whose veins there frequently flowed Chinese blood, like a permanent curse from the time when the Chinese had ravaged the Mongols' land.

And thus began the years of oblivion and loneliness for the once so fêted troubadour.

The men of the rather younger generation, who had been victims of "the black years" and the whole catastrophic decline of the past without any compensating feeling of having experienced its splendour, had become tired of listening to the songs and epics glorifying the past, and the growing youths turned their faces resolutely away from the dispirited old men to join their voices enthusiastically in the new marching songs, that were full of golden promises about the splendid future they themselves would build up.

SANGRUP became isolated, and was often abused by the younger members of his tribe; and when in fanatical loyalty to his calling he took up the gauntlet from the singers and expounders of the new songs, he had finally been imprisoned.

SANGRUP regarded his singing as a sacred calling, and the old songs as a sacred treasure for which he must find an heir, before he could go to his fathers with peace in his heart.

Even at quite a tender age it had been felt that he was predestined to become an interpreter of the treasury of song, and while he was still but a lad he had been taken to a celebrated troubadour, that the latter might test the genuineness of his gift and try his capacity to imitate the clear gurglings of streams, the gentle soughing of the wind in the rushes of the river-bank and the mystic echoes of eternity issuing from the invisible interior of the conch. When these and similar tests had fallen out to the master's satisfaction he had to undergo a long training in order to learn the many texts and melodies by heart, for written record of these there

[9] The older Khorchin Mongols in the Jasaktu *banner* use the expression Khara djil — "the black years", of the period 1911—13, when under Prince OTAI's leadership they fought their unhappy war of liberation against the modern-equipped soldiers of the Chinese Republic.

was none. He had also to learn which texts and melodies were suitable for the solemn occasions when the praises of high gods, proud heroes and famous horses were to be sung, which should be used when the cup of pleasure went the rounds, and which songs were in harmony with the still hours round the camp-fires of long winter evenings, when the hearts of the sitters should be warmed with the nostalgic strains of home-sickness and love.

SANGRUP had also had to learn to construct the traditional four-stringed "4-eared" violin and the two-stringed *khuur,* and he had been trained in the mysteries of acoustics by studying the sound-effects that the wind could coax from the hollow interiors of human and animal skulls.

Little by little, as SANGRUP began to realize that my interest in his talent and his lore was sincere, his at first slightly mistrustful helpfulness turned into intimate candour, and the aversion he had first felt for my modern recording apparatus was completely dissipated when I succeeded in getting him to understand its real purpose.

SANGRUP had never doubted that a coming generation would seek its way back to the old song-treasury of the people, and now it began to dawn upon him that with the aid of my mystical machinery he would be able to preserve the precious heritage in safety through an evil time, until Mongols should once again have an ear and a feeling for the tones that were of the same origin as themselves. At last he had found the solution he had so long sought, that would enable him to return to his honoured fathers without the heritage that had been entrusted to him being irrevocably lost.

SANGRUP took me to the last of the old-time Khorchin Mongols; and thanks to the great influence he wielded among these old men, whom life had made both mistrustful and dispirited, I came into possession of a representative collection of the old folk-songs, that they would perhaps otherwise not have entrusted to me, but taken with them in silence to the grave.

As the singers that we employed were aged and often toothless, so that their diction was not all that could be desired, SANGRUP clearly understood the importance of getting the texts of the recorded songs written down in correct and beautiful Mongolian, and as he himself could not write he helped me to get hold of a capable copyist to perform this work at his own dictation.

The continual journeys with the heavy and sensitive equipment through the difficult country took both time and energy, but the consciousness of the importance of our mission inspired us both with renewed strength and patience.

When at last we were approaching the north-west frontier of the old Khorchin country towards the Barga district, it seemed, however, as if the strange force that had hitherto driven the feeble old troubadour began to ebb; and when we tried to get into touch with the Barga tribes, whose customs and songs were strange to him, he gave up. The old man was unwilling once again to leave behind all the refound memories from the happy days of his youth, and one fine September morning he asked if I would agree to his turning back to die in the mountains of his native district at the foot of the "Bayan Jiruken", the rich heart of the Jasaktu country.

The loss of SANGRUP, "the All-knowing", was in the succeeding days so keenly felt by me that I began to doubt the continued success of my work; but my Mongolian star was still in the ascendant, and SANGRUP had many successors, who all furthered my work. That I have lingered in my account of SANGRUP more than in the case of his successors is due to the fact that in my mind he remains as a symbol of all that I sought, and all that I learned to love in the Mongolian wilderness.

But the others, too, I remember with pleasure: ÖLJEI TOKTAKHU, the professional troubadour from the Jalait tribe, whose whole life had been one long journey in the service of song, and who still remembered his native soil as the free steppe-land that it had been on the occasion of his last visit twenty years earlier. The Jalait tribe, whose grazing grounds are situated to the north-east of those of the Khorchin tribe, separated from the latter in the beginning of the 17th century. — They are probably descendants of the Jelair Mongols, a tribe that was known in the time of CHINGGIS KHAN. The Chinese colonization of their country began about 35 years ago, and most of their steppes have now been transformed into Chinese fields. — ÖLJEI TOKTAKHU gave me nine characteristic songs, that I appreciated so highly that I offered him a good round sum for every day that he consented to remain in my service. But one morning both the singer and his instrument had disappeared from the camp, although I was owing him for what he had already given me. Perhaps I had wounded the dignity of the poor troubadour by assessing his songs in terms of filthy lucre, or perhaps it was only his restless nomad blood, driving him farther on the life-long wandering towards the goal from which his swan-song should resound.

TEMURBAGAN gave me three of the songs of the Kharchin tribe. This tribe is descended in part, presumably, from the Khitan and Nuchen Tartars who between the 10th and the 13th centuries established independent states in North China under the dynastic names of Liao and Chin (Kin). The princes of the Kharchin tribe are called Tabunang (son-in-law), because they, unlike all other Mongol chieftains, are descended neither from CHINGGIS KHAN nor his brothers, but from one of the daughters of the great ruler. Most of the original grazing grounds of the tribe have now been colonized by the Chinese. Large numbers of the Kharchin Mongols have migrated to other parts of Mongolia, and the remainder of the population are losing their old nomad culture and even their own language.

Then there was SEMEN, the shy little woman from Jasaktu, who esteemed the songs she sang for me so highly that she could only sing them when clad in the full ceremonial dress of her tribe.

In order to reach Hailar I had to traverse the Barga district, that is squeezed in between Siberia, North Mongolia and Manchuria. Barga has approached now one, and now the other of the two last-mentioned states, according to the historical development in this difficult frontier-district, without, however, ever quite losing a certain administrative independence, that has often amounted to autonomy.

The name Barga comes from the old tribal name Barak, that is still used to designate certain groups in Chahar that have emigrated from Barga.

The first advance of Cossack bands towards the Baikal district in Siberia coincided with the rising power of the Manchus in the Kirin area, and as the South and East Siberian tribes felt more nearly related with the Tungusian Manchus than with the rude and ravaging Cossacks from the hitherto unknown west, a number of them began to drift eastward. After the Manchus had taken China they set about ordering the confused conditions in North Manchuria; and when the most advanced of the Cossack bands had been driven out of the country an agreement was reached with them by which the frontier was fixed along the water-shed running north of the River Amur. As a link in their endeavour to strengthen and stabilize the new frontier, the Manchus enlisted a number of warriors from northern Manchuria, transferring them to Barga; to this same district were also sent the refugees from Siberia who had succeeded in entering before the frontier had been fixed. These warriors were formed into 8 *banners,* in accordance with Manchurian military organization. In order to distinguish these 8 *banners* from the Chahars' 8 *banners* the two were called respectively the "outer" and the "inner" *banners.* The men who were enlisted in Barga's 8 outer *banners* were taken from the Buriat, Solon, Chipchin and Ölet tribes, which are all represented in Collection 2. —

The first *Buriats* came to Barga in the beginning of the 17th century, and their numbers were added to several times in the sequel by new migrations from their home-country round about Lake Baikal, as it became progressively Russianized. The last migration took place as late as the 1920's, when the Soviets tried to suppress their religion and their traditions, and to cut down still more the little freedom of movement that still remained to them. Among the latest arrivals there are people with Russian military and academic training, and many of these perform valuable service for the Japanese, in the hope of later enlisting the latter's help in winning back their native soil and their lost liberty.

Unlike the Buriats, who are of pure Mongolian race, both the Solon and the Chipchin peoples are of more or less Tungusian origin.

The Solons consider themselves to be more nearly related to the Manchus, and together with the Daghurs and the Fish-skin Tartars they are called "New Manchus". The Solons in Barga were transferred from Tsitsihar in 1738 as a punishment for "wild and unruly" behaviour, and on the same occasion 16 "squadrons" of Solons were sent to Chahar, where they were distributed, with 2 "squadrons" to each of the 8 "civilized" Chahar *banners.*

The Solons preserved their shaman cult in a purer form than any of the surrounding tribes; and even in Chakhar, where in 16 small communities they have lived in isolation from one another and surrounded by lamaistic tribes for more than 200 years, this mystical faith has retained its hold right up to the threshold of our modern times. In order to curb their wild temperament the Manchus had magnificent lama temples erected in the parts of the country inhabited by them, and the Solons have been obliged officially to profess the lama faith, with its peace-propaganda. But all the priests in their lama temples in Barga are either Buriats or Tibetans, and the new doctrine has never taken root in their minds.

To the west of the Hsingan Mountains the Solons have been strongly Mongolized; they speak Mongolian, besides their original mother-tongue, and they have in many points become different from their ethnically related kinsmen on the Nonni River. In 1928 I met people in Eastern Turkistan who were descended from Solon *banner* soldiers who at the beginning of the last century were transported here. They had retained the language of the tribe as well as other characteristics in a higher degree than their kinsmen in the home-country itself.

The Solons have always been known as brave fighters and skilful archers; but their numbers are rapidly decreasing on account of moral degeneration — a consequence of their lack of desire or ability to adapt themselves to the new era that is now dawning on their formerly so isolated haunts.

The Chipchin tribe that came to the Imperial hunting parks in Jehol from North Manchuria was transferred at the beginning of the 18th century to Barga. They themselves allege that they are related to the Buriats, but they are much more primitive than the latter in their way of life.

The Ölet Mongols in Barga belonged originally to a West Mongolian people that one finds distributed in groups and tribes from the Altai Mountains in Outer Mongolia right across Eastern Turkistan and into the Kuku Nor district in Tibet. In the 17th century they created a West Mongolian empire that ruled over the whole of Turkistan. They ravaged the countryside from Tibet to the River Volga and would have defeated the Khalkha Mongols if the latter had not been helped by the Manchus. The Ölet group now in Barga is descended from prisoners of war that the Manchus brought back from Turkistan in 1732.

Barin is one of the few tribes that have kept their name unchanged since the time of CHINGGIS KHAN.

Out of fear of the Chakhar Khan LIKDAN, to whom for a short period they were obliged to submit, the tribe entered in 1619 into an alliance with the Manchus.

In 1626, however, they broke this treaty in order to put themselves under the protection of the Ming government. After a Manchurian punitive expedition had broken the resistance of the Barin tribe it was once more exposed to LIKDAN'S plundering methods, and their chieftains had to seek refuge in the Khorchin country, until in 1626 they once more formed an alliance with the Manchus.

The Tumet tribe came presumably from North Mongolia, when in the 15th century they settled in the sterile Ordos Desert. Under the leadership of the great ALTAN KHAN the tribe moved to the rich country round about Kuku Khoto, and from here they made many plundering expeditions against China. In his old age ALTAN KHAN encouraged the introduction and spreading of lamaism in Mongolia (1577—78); and he founded the famous library that in 1926 was destroyed by Chinese soldiers.

The present chieftain is a direct descendant of ALTAN KHAN through 13 generations.

ALTAN KHAN's grandson moved with a small part of the tribe to Manchuria, and it is from this Tumet group that the Tumet song in Collection 2 derives (melody No. 73).

A number of the melodies in this collection were recorded in the vicinity of Hailar and Hsinking. Both of these towns, in their capacity of Mongolian administrative centres, are meeting places for members of several different tribes, and it was thus in several cases impossible to obtain satisfactory data concerning the home-country of the recorded melodies. The predominant element in the country around Hailar are Daghurs, who, as has already been mentioned in connection with Solons and Fish-skin Tartars, constitute a group referred to as "New Manchus". The language of the Daghurs is a mixture of Manchurian and Mongolian, but most of the men master the written form of both these languages. The Daghurs themselves state that they are descendants of a people that was subject to KHABTU KHASAR. They have long been known for their intelligence and scholarship, thanks to which they are often found in influential positions. They are rich and courteous and receptive for new impulses, without for this reason renouncing the essentials of their own culture. The present empress of Manchukuo is a daughter of a Daghur family from Hailar.

Hsinking, the new capital of Manchukuo, is situated on one of the steppes that until recently belonged under the administration of the Gorlos tribe.

The Gorlos tribe is mentioned already in annals from the time of CHINGGIS KHAN, where it is related that its members rose repeatedly in revolt against this ruler, until he marched against them to subdue them. CHINGGIS KHAN was met by the Gorlos chieftain NARAN KHAN at the head of 20,000 warriors, who were thoroughly defeated, NARAN KHAN himself being taken prisoner.

Together with a number of other tribes the Gorlos people constituted the federation that was led by KHABTU KHASAR. In the Mongolian annals Gorlos chieftains often appear as leaders of great Mongolian armies.

The Gorlos tribe is believed to be partly of Nuchen-Tartar origin, and thus related with the Manchus with whom they concluded a treaty in 1624. Their country, that is situated to the east of that of the Khorchin tribe, was formerly inhabited by Khitans. The population is well-to-do, very national and progressive-minded.

Large parts of their steppe have now been transformed to farming country, and the population has been to some extent converted to Chinese ways.

Fig. 1. The head of Jönung Khara Mori usually placed as decoration on the Mongolian *khil-khuur*.

Instruments of the kind used in the recording of the melodies occurring in this work have been brought home both to the Ethnographic Department of the Danish National Museum and to the Ethnographic Museum in Stockholm, where Dr Emsheimer has had the opportunity of pursuing the studies upon which his description of the instruments in the following chapter is based.

These old instruments, that were once manufactured by Mongolian musicians, and of which Mongols state that they are copies of original Mongol types, are now being replaced by machine-made instruments of Russian, Chinese and Japanese origin.

The old Mongols still tell of Argasun Khuurchi, Argasun the *Khuur* Player, who was Chinggis Khan's favourite troubadour, and a letter has been traced that the Mongol Argun Khan of Persia wrote to Philip the Fair of France, in which it is mentioned that the bearer of the letter was Argun's *khuur* player. The two *khuur* players mentioned probably strummed upon the same kind of *khuur* centuries ago as has been used for the recording of a number of the melodies included in this collection, that is considered by the Mongols as the harmonious attendant of Mongolian song.

An old Mongol friend from Chakhar once told me that when the last "horse-head violin" disappears, the old Mongol music will become mute, and when I began to ask him upon what he based this conviction, he related to me the legend of the first *khil-khuur* and of the origin of the Mongolian song:

Far in the north lies Bogdo Kure, "God's Monastery", that was once a Mecca for all Mongols, also for us here. But one must ride farther north, a journey of forty days, before one comes to the mountain Jasaktu Ul. The sacred mountain is visible a long way off, but one cannot reach it, for it is surrounded by swarms of small poisonous insects that kill all who try to approach it or leave it.

The ruler of the mountain is a mighty lion, but it is also unable to leave the sacred precincts of the mountain. Jasaktu Ụl is extensive and wonderful with snow-clad peaks and luxuriant valleys, and in these graze Erdenin naiman mori, "The eight precious horses". They are all stallions, and seven of them are fat and splendid to see. The eighth horse is thin and miserable-looking, it hangs its head and its ribs can be counted. Nonetheless, it is swifter and more enduring than any of the others. Its name is Jönung Khara Mori.

On certain nights twenty-eight twinkling stars fall down to the earth to absorb its fertility. As shooting stars they fall through the dark night, but when they reach the earth they are transformed to young warriors clad in sparkling gold coats of mail.

Twenty of them are mounted on horseback, but eight sink down on the Jasaktu Mountain, for the eight horses belong to them. And here they mount Erdenin Naiman Mori, after which they join their twenty brothers out on the steppe. Now all together gallop about on the earth as long as the night lasts, and wherever their horses set their hooves beauty and exuberance grow up.

In good time before dawn they reascend to their places in the night sky, sparkle for a short while as morning stars, to be eclipsed soon by the daylight until the night comes again.

But with the leader of the twenty-eight riders, he who is mounted upon the thin but swift one of the eight horses of the Jasaktu Mountain, a young shepherdess from the west becomes enamoured, and the young star-prince returns her love. All the late nighthours that his starry brothers use to shine as morning stars in the sky are spent by him in the tent of his beloved. But this lay far from the Jasaktu Mountain, and it was the extra riding that this entailed that caused his horse, Jönung Khara Mori, to become thinner and thinner, without, however, abating any of his swiftness. Every night the star-prince and his Mongol maid slept in each other's arms; but each morning when the girl awoke she found herself alone — both the prince and his steed had disappeared, and not even the marks of the horse's hooves were visible in the sand.

This astonished the shepherdess, who was accustomed both to awake at the slightest noise and to track horses, so she tried to stay awake, and had her best horse in readiness to be able to follow the prince and find out his refuge. But in vain, the prince and his horse vanished like a gust in the night, and with such speed that no mortal horse could follow them.

The next time the Mongol maid was visited by her prince she waited until he had gone to sleep, and then went out to his mysterious horse to examine it. She now discovered that the thin horse had small wings, that lay folded behind each of his legs, and in the hope that if she robbed him of his wings she might be able to keep her lover she cut them off.

But when she awoke the next morning she was again alone, — and the star-prince and his steed never returned.

After the flying prince had been rushing through space on his marvellous horse for a time, on the way to his star, he discovered that his otherwise so indefatigable steed was beginning to show signs of exhaustion. And finally he fell down with his steed in a great and desolate desert, where the horse sank to the ground and expired. In despair over the loss of his marvellous steed, and persuaded that he would now never again be able to reach either his star or his beloved, who both dwelt so far away that one could not reach them on an ordinary horse, he began to caress his dead steed. And between his stroking hands, while the tears fell from his eyes, a miracle took place. The dead horse was transformed into the first *khilkhuur,* an instrument that was ornamented on top with his horse's head; and the horse's mane and the hairs of his tail, that he had been holding crushed in his hands, were changed into sounding strings.

Just at that moment the sun was rising over the distant horizon of sand, the first sunrise the star-prince had beheld on earth, and his home-star was eclipsed in the light of the new day. Moved by the beauty of the hour, he touched the strings of his instrument, and upon his lips words were born, that followed the strange vibrations of the strings — and this was the first of the Mongols' songs. Thereafter he wandered over the Mongolian steppes, over the mountains and deserts, and everywhere he sang and played about his dead horse, his distant star and his lost love. And wherever he roamed the Mongols flocked to listen to him; and so entranced were they that after his disappearance they made copies of his *khil-khuur,* and upon these they played his songs, and quite new songs, that were inspired by what they had heard him sing.

And this is why the most dearly loved instrument of the Mongols is still decorated with Jönung Khara Mori's head, and why their songs, or the best and the oldest of them, are melancholy strains that sing of horses, love, and distant, unattainable stars.

Fig. 2. "Erdenin Naiman Mori", the eight precious horses, drawn after the painting on the harpe. Pl. VI 2.

Before I conclude this rambling introduction to Collection 2, I must give myself the pleasure of expressing my deeply felt gratitude to the persons and institutions without whose enthusiastic interest and kind help I should never have succeeded in getting this collection published.

My former chief, Dr Sven Hedin, was the first European to take an interest in this part of my work, and it was thanks to his experienced guidance and never-failing helpfulness that I ventured to set about the task. That the book can make its appearance at the present juncture is due to the fact that Dr Hedin had it prepared by Dr E. Emsheimer while I was still occupied in Mongolia with getting together the material for Collection 3.

I must also express my thanks to Dr Emsheimer, who undertook the difficult task of writing down the melodies from my gramophone records in accordance with our system of notation.

The collection could never have turned out anything like so satisfactory as it has done if I had not had the two modern recording apparatuses that the Swedish Broadcasting Corporation placed at my disposal. Director Anders Dymling's motivation for this priceless gift was that the cultural results of my expedition would certainly prove worth this contribution, and I hope that they have not disappointed the former chief of the Swedish Broadcasting Corporation or his many listeners.

I also want to express my deepfelt gratitude to Mr. J. von Utfall of The Technical Department of The Swedish Broadcasting Corporation who was untiring in his efforts to comply with all my wishes in constructing a recording outfit which in such a superior way stood the test of a very trying expedition.

At a juncture when the material for this book was already prepared, but the expected funds for its publication were not forthcoming, owing to the world-situation that arose, I addressed myself to the Danish Rask-Ørsted Fund, that kindly undertook the considerable expense of publication. It is a source of particular gratification to me that the costs for the printing of this book are being borne by my own country.

The Mongolian song-texts included here have been translated by Dr. K. Grønbech, who was my philological collaborator on my last expedition. In order not to delay the publication of the book, only those songs have been included that Dr Grønbech's heavy burden of work has so far left him time to translate; but it is our intention to publish all the song-texts with their translations in due course.

Lodai Lama from Khalkha Mongolia, who for several months was my fellow-traveller, has painted the frontispiece, which is an illustration to a Mongol song.

My warmest and most heartfelt thanks, however, must be tendered to the Mongolian singers and musicians who gave me of their lore, and who so willingly helped me to record some of the treasures of old music whose guardians and interpreters they were. Many of these troubadours are now dead, and many of the songs will remain forever mute with them in Mongolia.

When in the spring of 1937 I took leave of Sangrup, the Khorchin tribe's last troubadour of the old school, he begged me to take good care of the treasury of song he had entrusted to me, so that it might be a blessing and a source of pleasure in the future, as it had been in the past, and I have tried to comply with his wish to the best of my ability.

SPECIMENS OF MONGOLIAN POETRY

TRANSLATED BY

K. GRØNBECH

At the time of recording the songs contained in this volume Mr. H. HASLUND-CHRISTENSEN also had the texts of the songs written down by some literate Mongol. From these transcripts Mr. W. A. UNKRIG attempted to reconstruct the actual wording of the songs. When, for the reasons stated by Mr. EMSHEIMER in his introduction, this experiment had to be abandoned, I was asked to furnish an English translation of a number of texts, so as to give a general idea of the kind of poetry embodied in the songs.

The following translations are meant as illustrations of some of the more important types of Mongolian songs, represented in this volume. As basis for the translation served notations of the songs, written down by the Mongols themselves immediately after they had been sung. A valuable help were the paraphrases of some of the songs prepared by Mr. H. HASLUND-CHRISTENSEN with the assistance of a young Khorchin girl.

The English versions follow the wording of the originals as closely as possible without unduly violating the normal English word-order and phraseology. Many, both lyrical and narrative Mongolian songs are however built on incidents, legendary or historical, ancient or modern, many of which happen to be unknown to the translator. Obscure passages are therefore frequently met with which could only be fully explained by Mongols who are familiar with the background of the song in question. Also some of the songs contain words that are unknown to our dictionaries. In such cases my translation represents only one among several possible renderings or just a plausible guess.

No attempt could be made to imitate such formal characteristics of the original as rhythm and alliteration, although the latter is a very prominent feature of the majority of the songs. In order to give the general reader some impression of the formal structure of Mongolian songs, I reproduce one of them (no. 70) in phonetic transcription. Attention should however be drawn to the fact that literary Mongolian does not in all respects give a very exact picture of the actual pronunciation, the modern dialects exhibiting a considerable number of contractions and droppings of both consonants and vowels, which has in course of time greatly reduced the number of syllables.

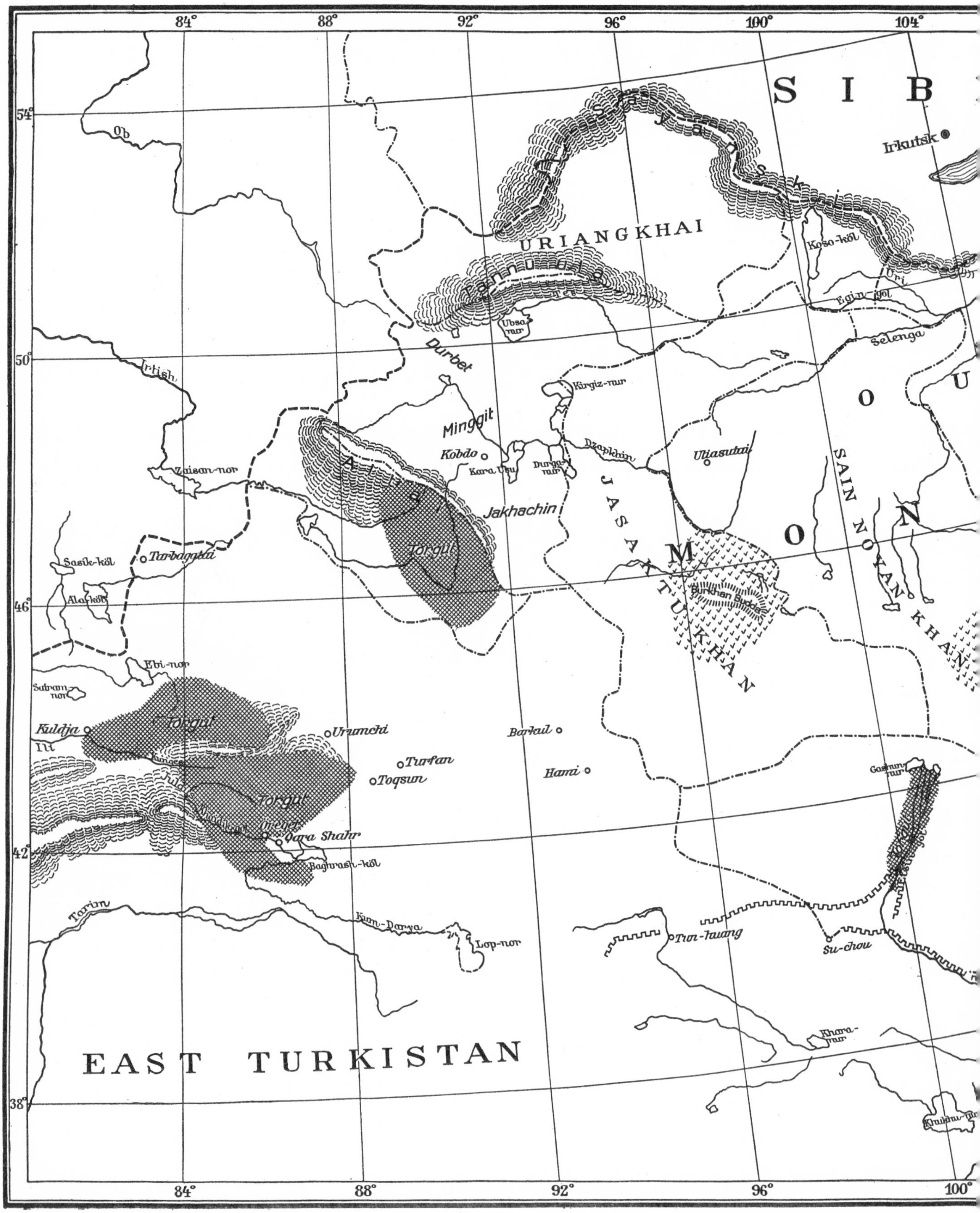

84°
88°
92°
96°
100°
104°
54°
50°
46°
42°
38°
S I B
Irkutsk
URIANGKHAI
Koso-köl
Ubsa-nur
Egin-gol
Selenga
Ob
Irtish
Durbet
Kirgiz-nur
Minggit
Kobdo
Kara Usu
Durga-nur
Dzapkhin
Uliasutai
O
U
SAIN NOYAN KHAN
N
O
M
JASAKTU KHAN
Jakhachin
Torgut
Zaisan-nor
Tarbagatai
Sasik-köl
Ala-köl
Ebi-nor
Kuldja
Ili
Torgut
Urumchi
Turfan
Toqsun
Barkul
Hami
Torgut
Qara Shahr
Baghrash-köl
Tarim
Kum-Darya
Lop-nor
Tun-huang
Su-chou
Khara-nur
EAST TURKISTAN

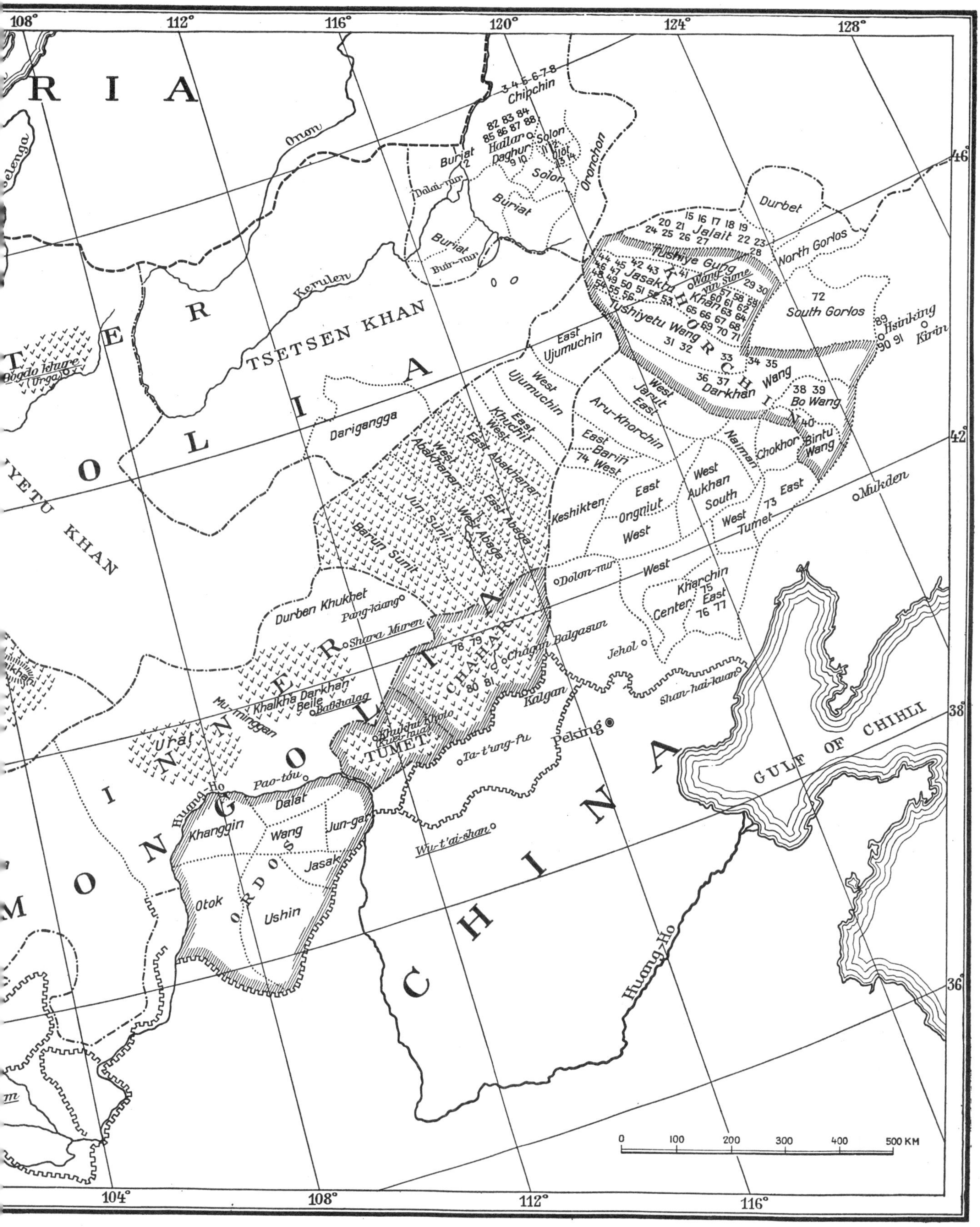

108°
112°
116°
120°
124°
128°
46°
42°
38°
36°
104°
108°
112°
116°
R I A
T E R
O L I A
M O N G O L I A
I N N E R
C H I N A
CHINA
TSETSEN KHAN
YETU KHAN
KHORCHIN
CHAHAR
TUMET
ORDOS
GULF OF CHIHLI
Onon
Kerulen
Selenga
Bogdo Khure (Urga)
Chipchin
Hailar
Buriat
Daghur
Solon
Ölöt
Oronchon
Dalai-nur
Buir-nur
Durbet
Jalait
Tushiye Gung
Jasaktu
Wang-yin Sume
Khan
Tushiyetu Wang
North Gorlos
South Gorlos
Hsinking
Kirin
Darkhan Wang
Bo Wang
Bintu Wang
Chokhor
Naiman
East Ujumuchin
West Ujumuchin
Dariganga
Aru-Khorchin
East Barin
West
East Jarut
West
Khuchit
West Abakhanar
East Abakhanar
Jun Sunit
Barun Sunit
East Abaga
West Abaga
Keshikten
East Ongniut West
West Aukhan
South
West Tumet East
Mukden
Dolon-nur
Kharchin
Center
East
West
Jehol
Durben Khukhet
Pang-kiang
Shara Muren
Chagan Balgasun
Khalkha Darkhan Beile
Batkhalag
Mu-minggen
Urat
Kalgan
Peking
Shan-hai-kuan
Kuei-hua
Khukhu Khoto
Ta-t'ung-fu
Pao-t'ou
Huang Ho
Dalat
Khanggin
Wang
Jun-gar
Jasak
Otok
Ushin
Wu-t'ai-shan
0 100 200 300 400 500 KM

The Mongolian scholars, who compare the translations with the facsimiles of the Mongolian texts, will need to be informed that the translator was able to work from the original notations of the scribes. Most of these transcripts were hastily noted down in very cursive writing and are unfit for reproduction. Mr. H. HASLUND-CHRISTENSEN therefore had them copied at Köke Khoto (Kuei-hua-ch'eng), prov. of Sui-yuan, North China, by two Chakhar Mongols, both of the Bordered Red Banner; their Chinese names are Liu Chou-sien and He(ho) Min-chou respectively. Their clean copy, which was used as basis for the facsimiles reproduced in this volume, differs in some respects from the originals; the alterations introduced by them sometimes represent real improvements, but more often the opposite, consisting frequently of mere blunders or omissions. A detailed philological commentary would under these circumstances have been desirable, but would go too far beyond the scope of this publication. For these reasons the reader will have to take the translations on trust, based as they are on a better text than the one here reproduced.

56. THE WILLOWS OF BURIN KHAN.

The willows of Burin Khan
form the shade of the cloudy mountain.
The happiness of all Mongols
derives from the strength of Buddha's creed.

We (Mongols) of the rising sun,
We (Mongols) of the mountain showing through the mists,
We (Mongols) of the sprouting trees,
We (Mongols) of the (fresh-)smelling waters,

May we prosper for ten thousand ages;
Let us rally round (?) the ministers and ambans.[1]
May we thrive for a thousand ages;
Let us live in joy and happiness.

[1] Governor.

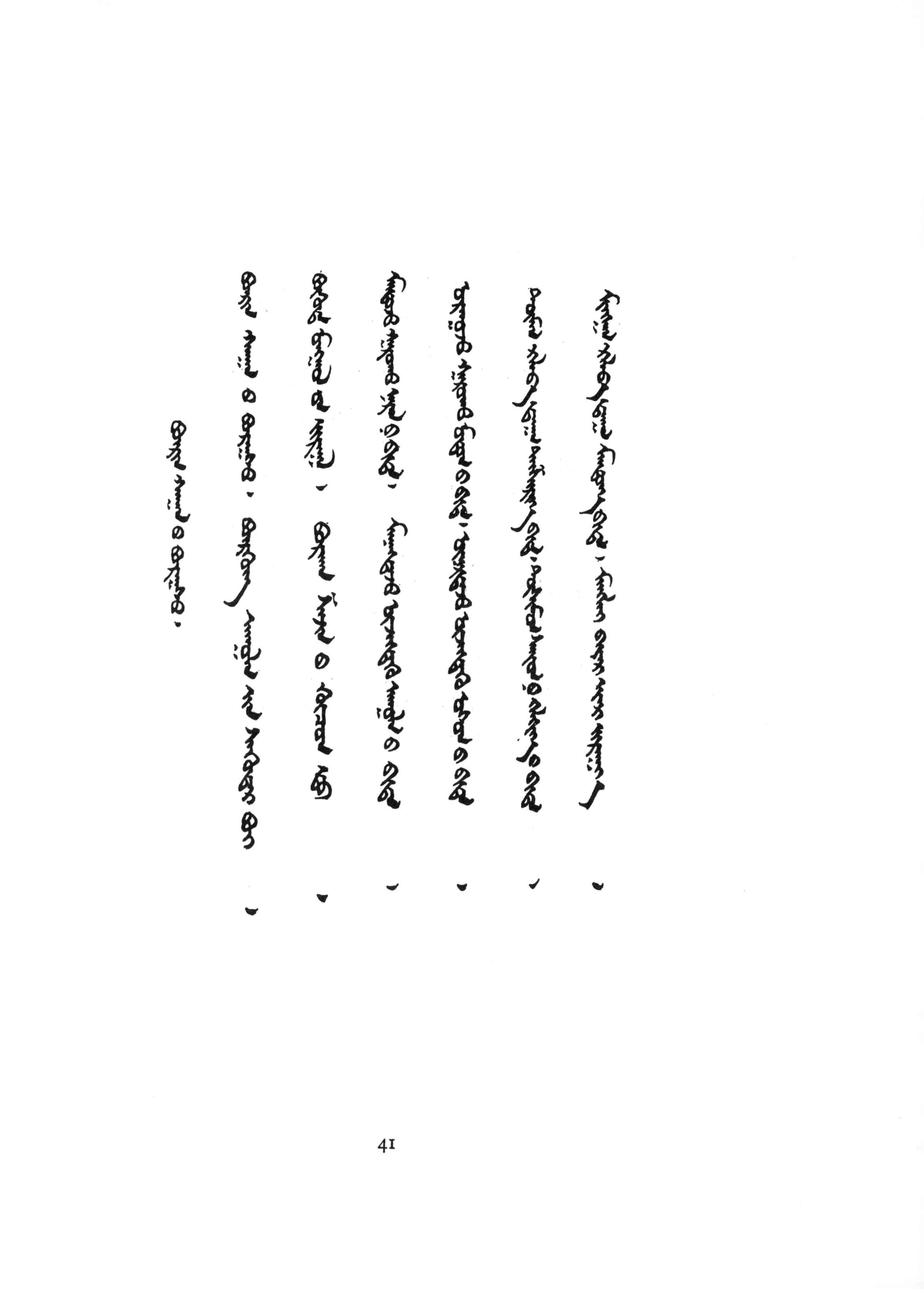

[illegible]

54. KHASAR CHINGGIS.[1]

The noble offspring of Khasar Chinggis,
The favoured kinsmen of the lord the Khan,
The guardian officers of the Government of Jade,
The foremost chiefs of the emperors are we Khorchin.

The foremost families
The dignified customs of the Dai-ching people.[2]
The Chin-Wangs of twofold rank
were from the very first found among us Khorchin.

The wooded range with its beautiful trees,
The Onon river with its beautiful course.
The people is clever and wise.
The one they revere is the holy lama.

Strong and faithful is (our) truthful soul,
Brave and resolute are the chiefs of the realm.
Immensely rich is our tribal land,
Happy and joyful are we Khorchin

Unyielding is (our) truthful soul,
unabated (our) unflinching valour.
Our materialized deliverer is the image of the Buddha with relics (inside)
The one we contemplate and revere is the holy lama.

1 One of the brothers of Chinggis Khan. From him descend the chiefs of the Khorchin tribe in Eastern Mongolia. The Khorchin Mongols were the most important supporters in the 17th century of the growing Manchu power, and subsequently under the Manchu dynasty of China they therefore enjoyed numerous privileges. Their chiefs repeatedly intermarried with the Manchu emperors, several of whom were sons of Khorchin mothers.

2 The Manchu dynasty.

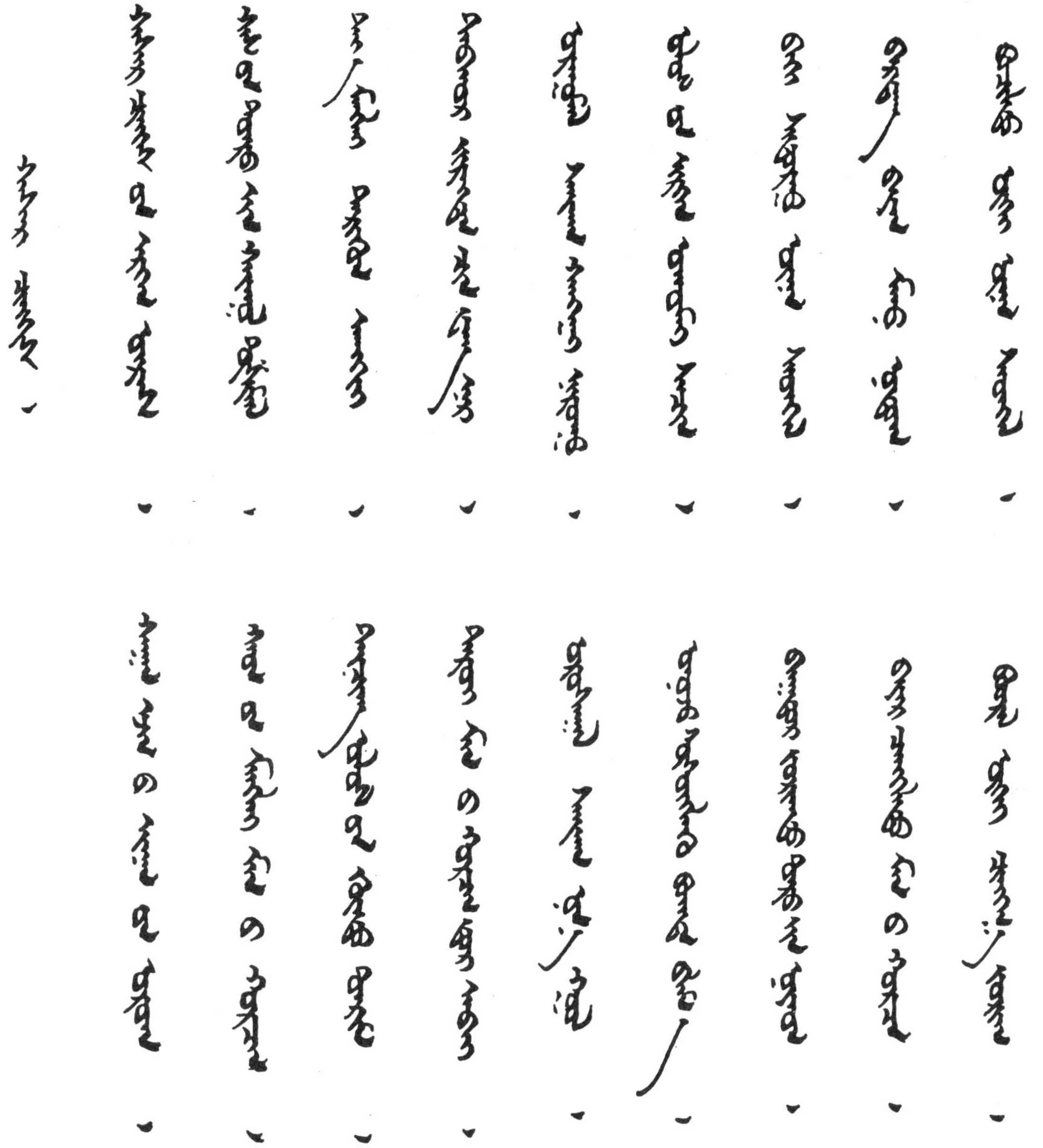

Our mail-clad warriors are fiery and straight,
Our laws and regulations are an inflexible force.
The customs of our temple festivals[1] and feasts are beautiful,
dignified customs of us Khorchin.

Skill in hunting, well-filled bags,
steeds, wine and meat,
tribute and subsidy;
Renowned and famous are we Khorchin.

The nobles of the realm, the Living Buddhas,
The officials and administrators are impeachably honest.
The ten thousand subjects are peaceful and quiet;
Perfectly happy are we Khorchin.

The rule of the emperor is strong and firm,
The descendants of Khabtu[2] are brave and awe-inspiring,
The soul of everybody is peaceful.
May the protection of the emperors be for ever extended.

1 Properly the serving service of the lamas.

2 Khabtu is another name of Khasar.

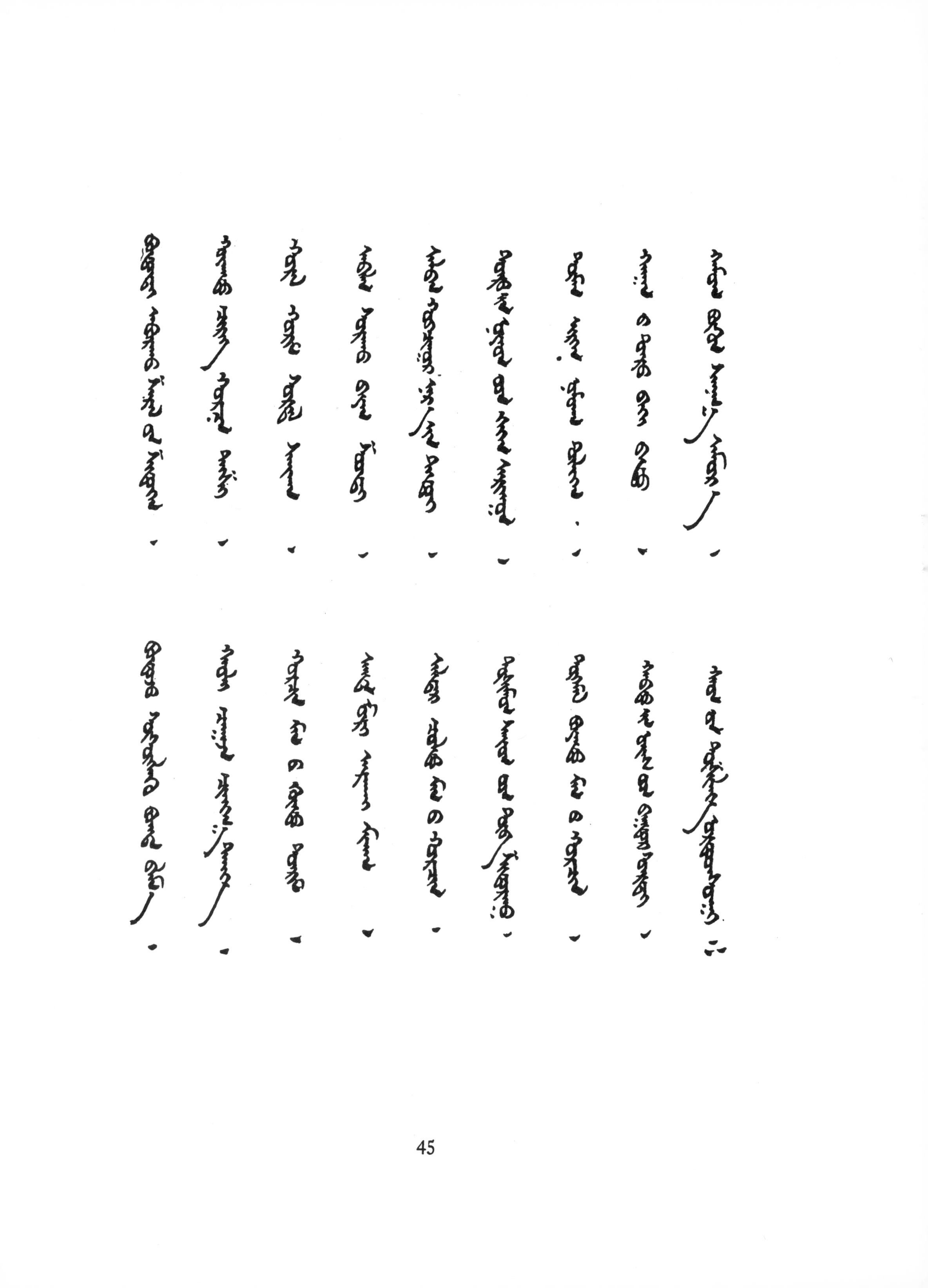

[illegible]
[illegible]
[illegible]
[illegible]
[illegible]
[illegible]
[illegible]
[illegible]

[illegible]
[illegible]
[illegible]
[illegible]
[illegible]
[illegible]
[illegible]
[illegible]

16. THE WINDS OF HEAVEN.

The winds of heaven shift and change,
your body will not live forever;
your mortal body has but its brief span of life.
May we, fast friends that have met, all live long and happily together!

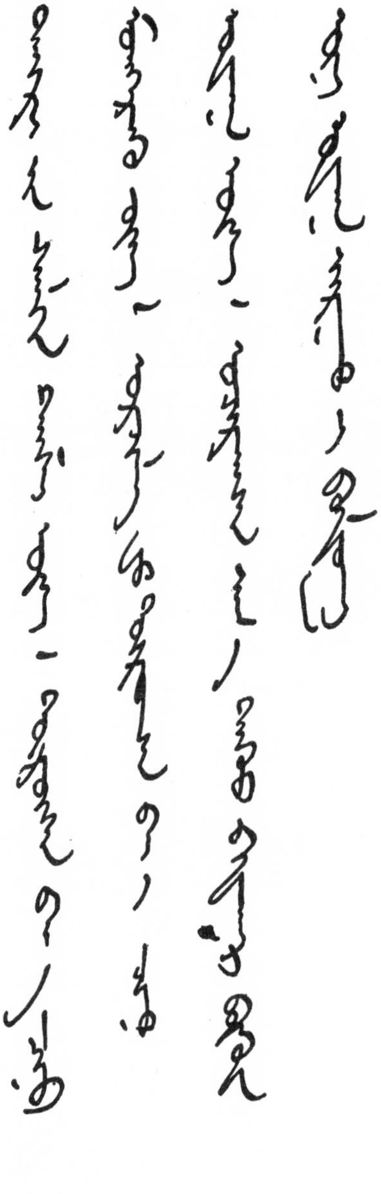

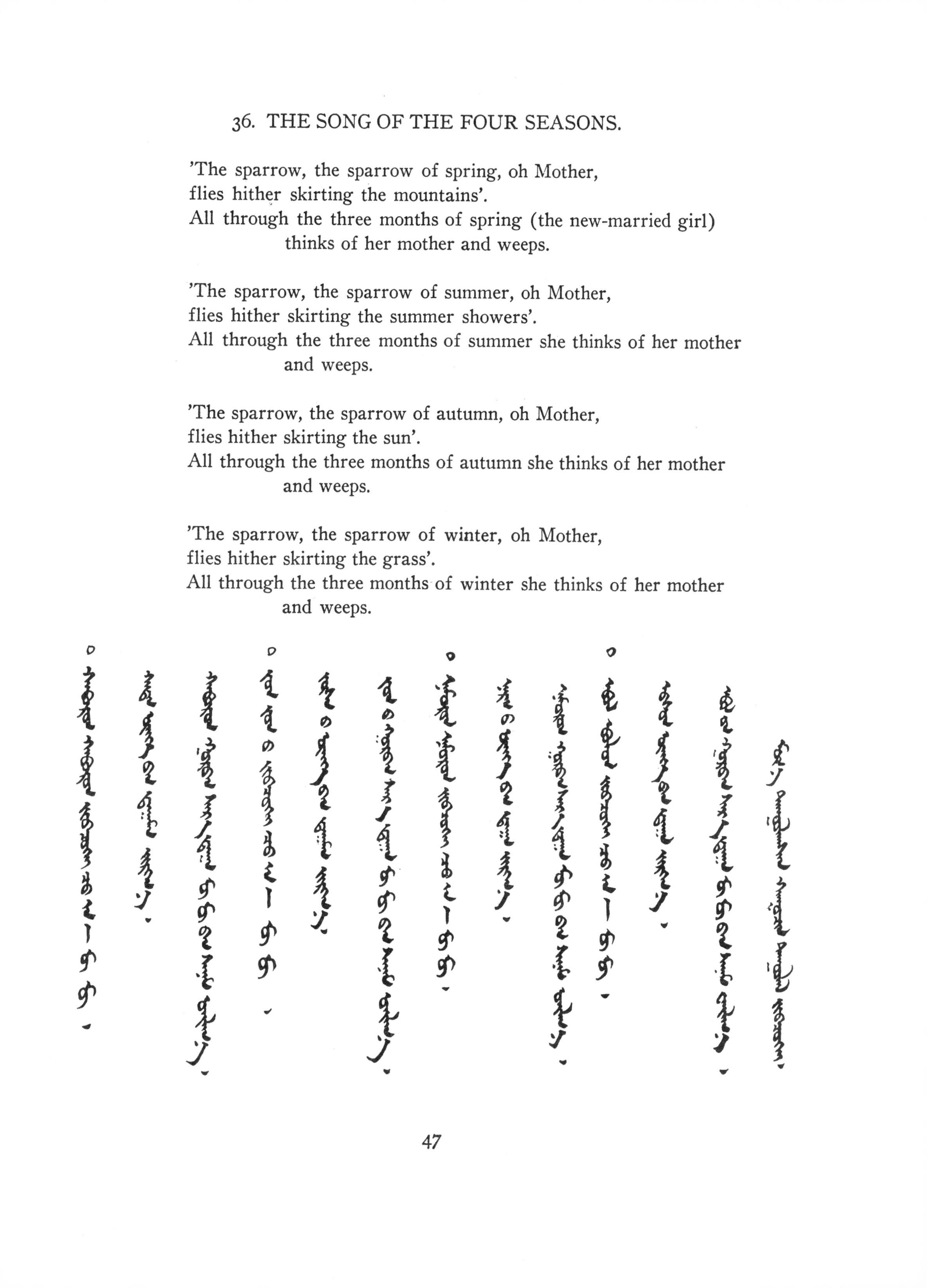

36. THE SONG OF THE FOUR SEASONS.

'The sparrow, the sparrow of spring, oh Mother,
flies hither skirting the mountains'.
All through the three months of spring (the new-married girl)
thinks of her mother and weeps.

'The sparrow, the sparrow of summer, oh Mother,
flies hither skirting the summer showers'.
All through the three months of summer she thinks of her mother
and weeps.

'The sparrow, the sparrow of autumn, oh Mother,
flies hither skirting the sun'.
All through the three months of autumn she thinks of her mother
and weeps.

'The sparrow, the sparrow of winter, oh Mother,
flies hither skirting the grass'.
All through the three months of winter she thinks of her mother
and weeps.

41. THE SMOKE OF INCENSE.

The smoke of incense diffuses richly in the temple hall;
countless novices of the temple offer up their incense-sticks and prostrate themselves.

On the border of the yellow steppe is the house of the Yellow Creed;[1]
there dwell our lama saints, devoted to their Holy Doctrine.

On the border of the grey steppe is the house of Buddha's teaching;
there dwell our lama saints, steeped in Buddha's law.

1 The now dominating sect of Lamaism, so called from the colour of the cap of its lama adherents. The sect was founded about 1400 by the Tibetan church-reformer Tsong-K'a-pa.

[illegible]

[illegible]

[illegible]

[illegible]

[illegible]

[illegible]

[illegible]

45. DOWN FROM THE HEIGHT.

When the clouds descend from on high, a storm is arising;
when you meditate in time, you will find it useful on a later day.
Buddha's teaching has subjugated death and birth.

When the clouds appear in the sky, a storm is approaching;
when you meditate on life, you will find it useful in the end.
How long shall I live on earth, when shall I offer up my prayers(?).

However high the hill, there is a path which has been climbed before,
however much the younger prince is fond of his daughter, he will have to
lead her to a foreign country (to be married).
However high the mountain, there is a path which has been climbed before;
though the emperor has a daughter-princess, she must end her days in a
foreign country.

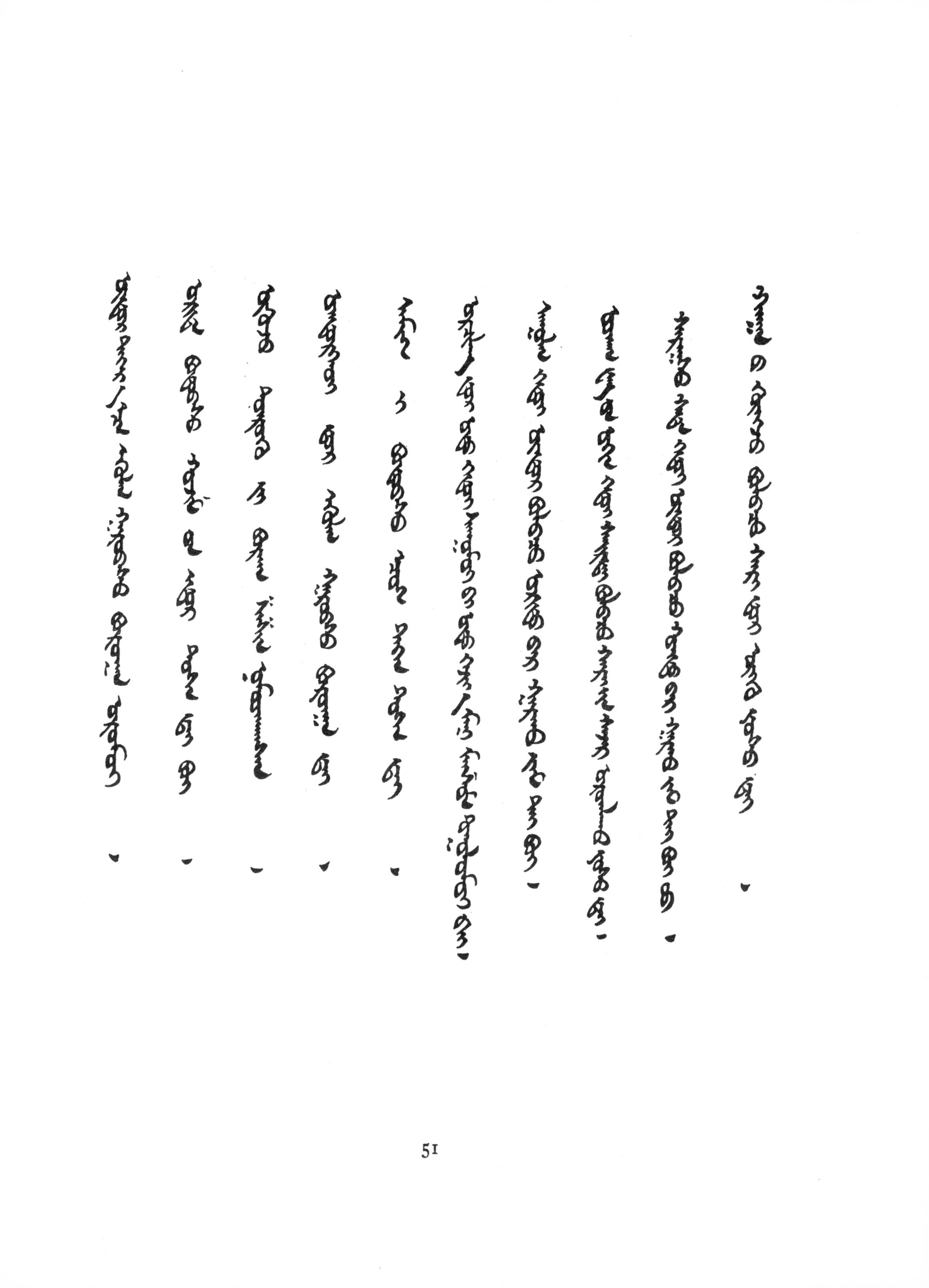

55. THE RICH HEART,[1] THE GREAT PRINCE OF JASAKTU.

The all-powerful mountain is the king of the waters,
  he looks like the all-encompassing Sumeru.[2]
The dancing king is like the Garuda bird,
  he conquers the cliff of the fat, poisonous snakes.

When I let my eyes rove over the mountain
  he looks like a lion on the catch.
When I climb upon the central peak,
  he is beautifully bright and clear.

He is the fountainhead of full ten thousand mountain streams,
  he is the god that bestows salmon without measure,
he sends timely rain for the flowers,
  he is the mountain of all-mastering foresight.

Tiger and wolf in the dells
  and men when they quarrel he curbs,
from the sheep and the cattle in the enclosure
  may he keep famine far away!

[1] Name of a mountain. [2] Mount Meru, the large mountain which according to Buddhist doctrine forms the centre of this world, round which are grouped the four continents and the eight islands.

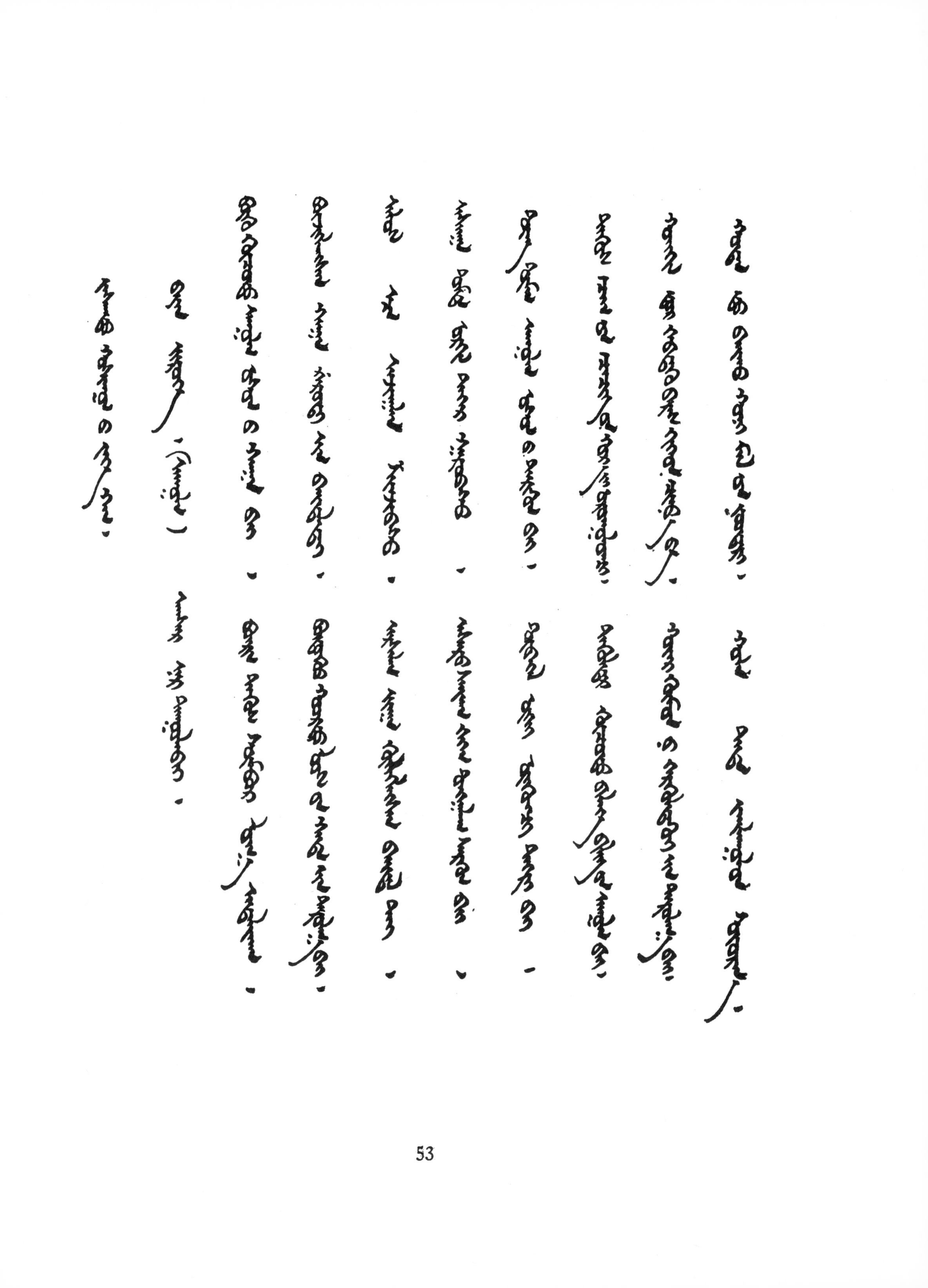

(May he send) luck to the well-fed horses and camels
  and to the sheep and cattle of the Five Banners.
He is the god that bestows salmon without stint.
  I bring offerings while your hearts rejoice.

The plains and valleys are wide,
  the breeze is cool and soft.
Ye rulers of my banner, the Jasaktu,
  I sing the praise of your bounty.

[illegible] ᠂ [illegible] ᠂

[illegible] ᠂ [illegible] ᠂

[illegible] ᠂ [illegible] ᠂

[illegible] ᠂ [illegible] ᠃

60. THE SLIM BLUE HORSE.

"The slim, blue horse, so sprightly in autumn.
— My old, grey mother I shall meet one happy day." —

"The piebald blue horse, so sprightly in winter.
— My aged, grey mother I shall meet in the happiness of health." —

"The appletree, the appletree, while you were making a cradle of it, Father,
in the third month of winter there is heavy suffering, Mother."

"The elmtree, the elmtree, while you were making a house of it, Father,
in the third month of spring there is heavy suffering, Mother."

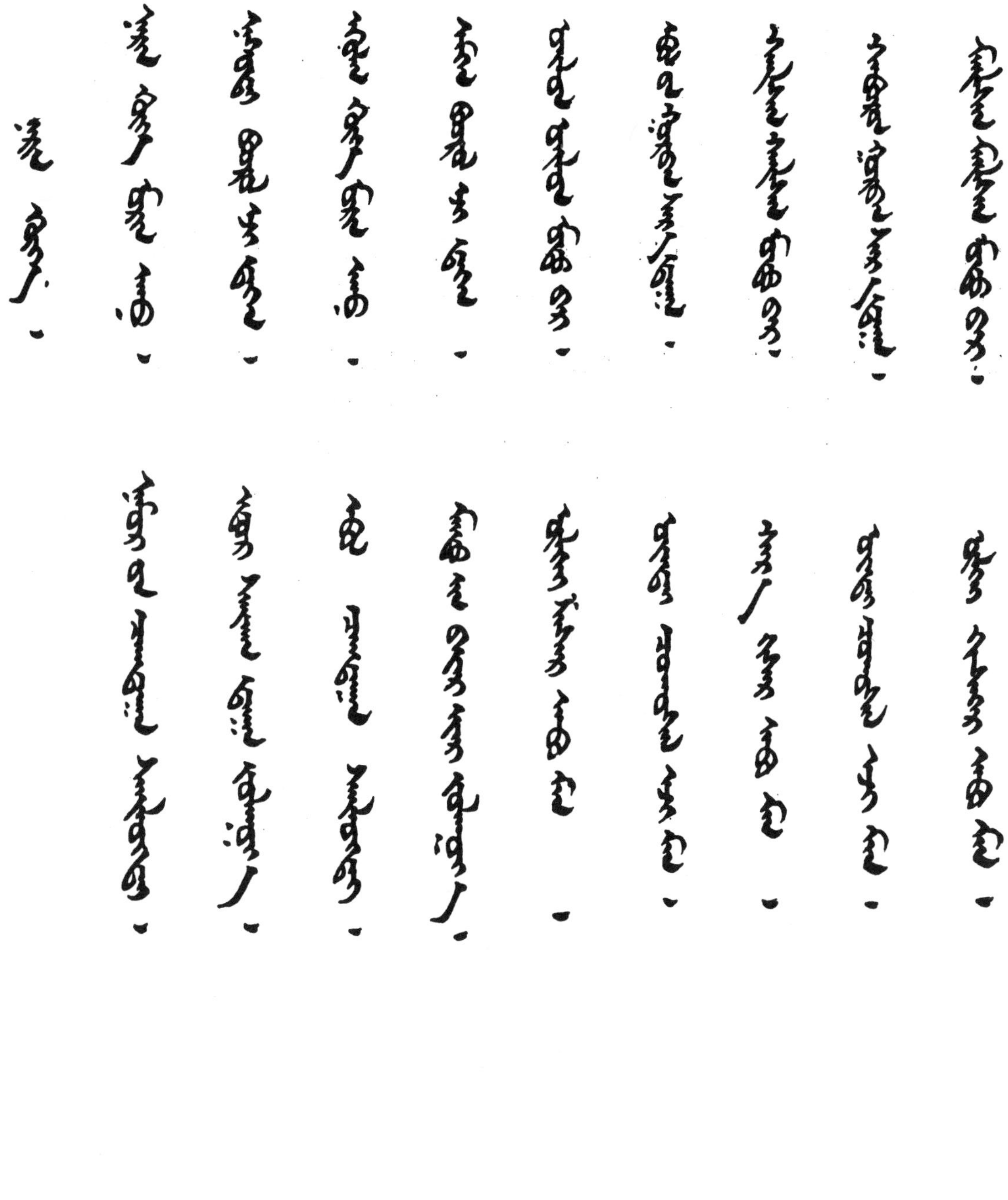

"The cypress, the cypress, while you were making a cradle of it, Father,
the flies and midges my mother chased away and killed."

The warbler of the Lake Ghanghan circles the Ghanghan and sings.
The girl that was given away in marriage to a far-away country thinks of her mother and sings.

[illegible]

[illegible]

[illegible]

68. THE EIGHT PARTS OF THE WORLD.

A song to the universe,[1] to the splendour of sun and moon,
the archer's shooting song, the drinking song of ye, old men,
a song of instruction to the young, a drinking song of the drunken old men.

Let us laugh and make merry in the world of this king,
let us dance and make merry in the empire of this king.

1 Literally: The Sumeru mountain of the eight islands of the world, on which see note above.

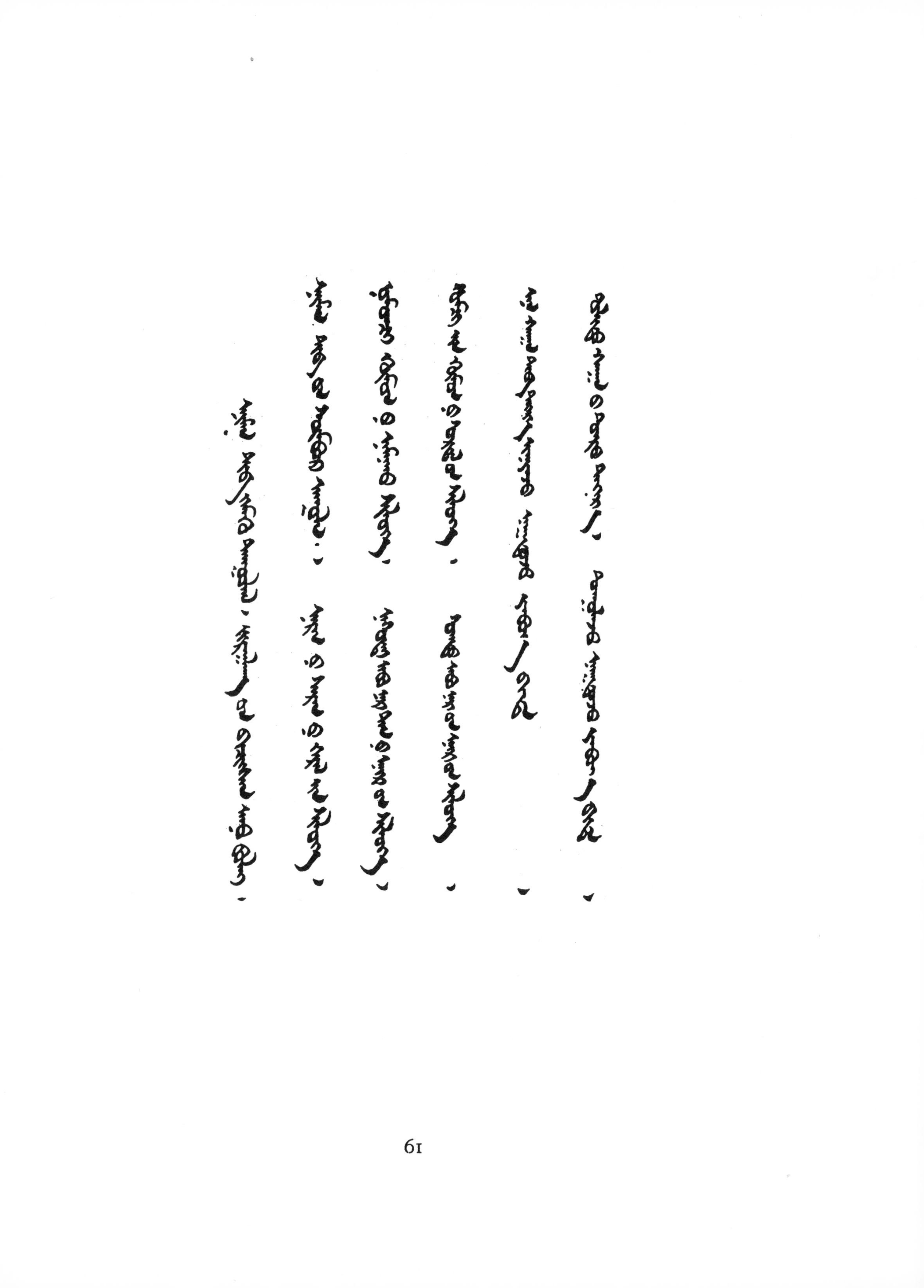

70. DAZZLINGLY WHITE.

(A song for the feast held in honour of the marriage-makers).
When it was time to gladden the resplendent heaven,
when small and great should be made to rejoice,

— The grass of Juilighai is the food of the antilope hinds —
I offered brandy, distilled on fruits, to the old men.

— The water of the well is the drink of the cattle of the tribe —
I offered wine in a cup to ye marriage-makers.

Seizing the young of the tiger is a thing hard to achieve,
teaching children of tender age is a thing hard to achieve.

Taking the young of the poisonous snake into one's lap is a thing hard to achieve,
teaching the children of the coming age is a thing hard to achieve.

In Mongolian this song reads as follows:[1]

Badarangghui tengri-yi
bagha yekhe khoyar-yi
Juilighai-yin ebesü
jimis-iyer neregsen sarakhun
Khudug-u usu bei
khuntagha-du khigsen sarakhun
Baras-un juljagha-yi
bagha üye-yin kheüked-yi
Khoortu moghai-yin joljagha-yi
khojim üyes-ün kheüked-yi
bayasghulju baikhui-yin üyes-dü,
jirghal-yi khijü baikhui-dur,
jür sogho-yin idegen bei,
abu-nar-daghan jogholbai.
khoshighu mal-dur umdaghan bei.
khuda-nar tan-daghan jogholbai.
bariju abukhui-dur berkhe,
surghaju khelekhüi-dür berkhe.
khormailaju abukhui-dur berkhe,
surghal abukhui-a berkhe.

[1] Sh, ch, j and y have their normal English value; kh is pronounced like German ch, while gh is a spirantic g. ü is a somewhat palatalized u.

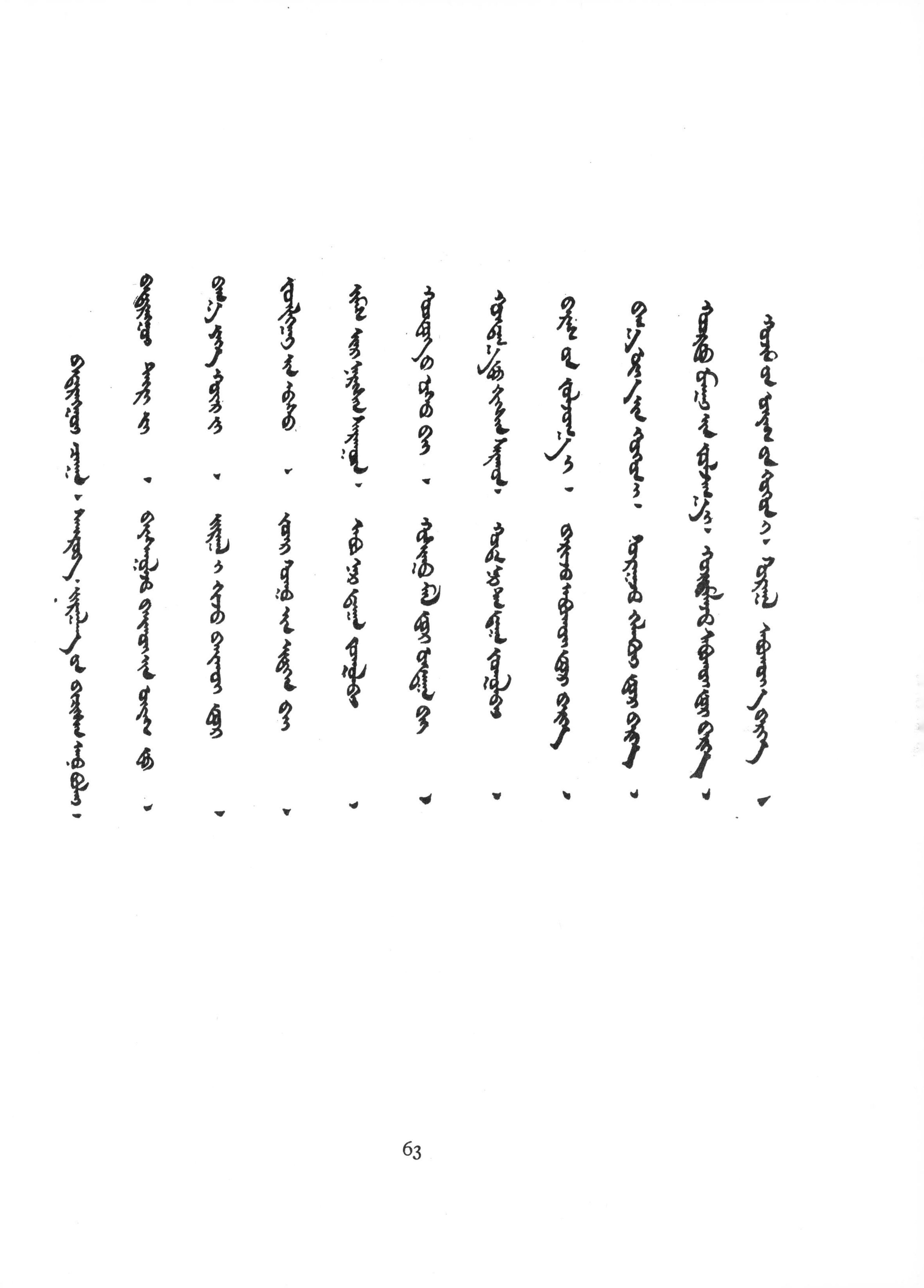

[illegible]

71. CHIMED BADMA.

(Chimed Badma has been given away in marriage to a man of the Durbet tribe far to the west, and now her elder brother sings:)

When I went on a journey to far away parts,
my little Chimed Badma remained in my tent;
when I returned from my journey to far away parts,
I gave my little Chimed Badma away in marriage.

When I went on a journey to countries remote,
my bonny Chimed Badma remained in my tent;
when I returned from my journey to countries remote,
I gave my bonny Chimed Badma away in marriage.

I bought her a red silk coat from the far away town.
To what point of the sky did I lead my young bonny Chimed Badma and give her away?

I bought her a blue silk coat from the shop in the town.
To what blue mountain did I lead my bonny sister Chimed Badma and give her away?

I bought her a white silk coat from the town of Shagjighai.
To what hazy mountain did I lead my bonny, pretty Chimed Badma and give her away?

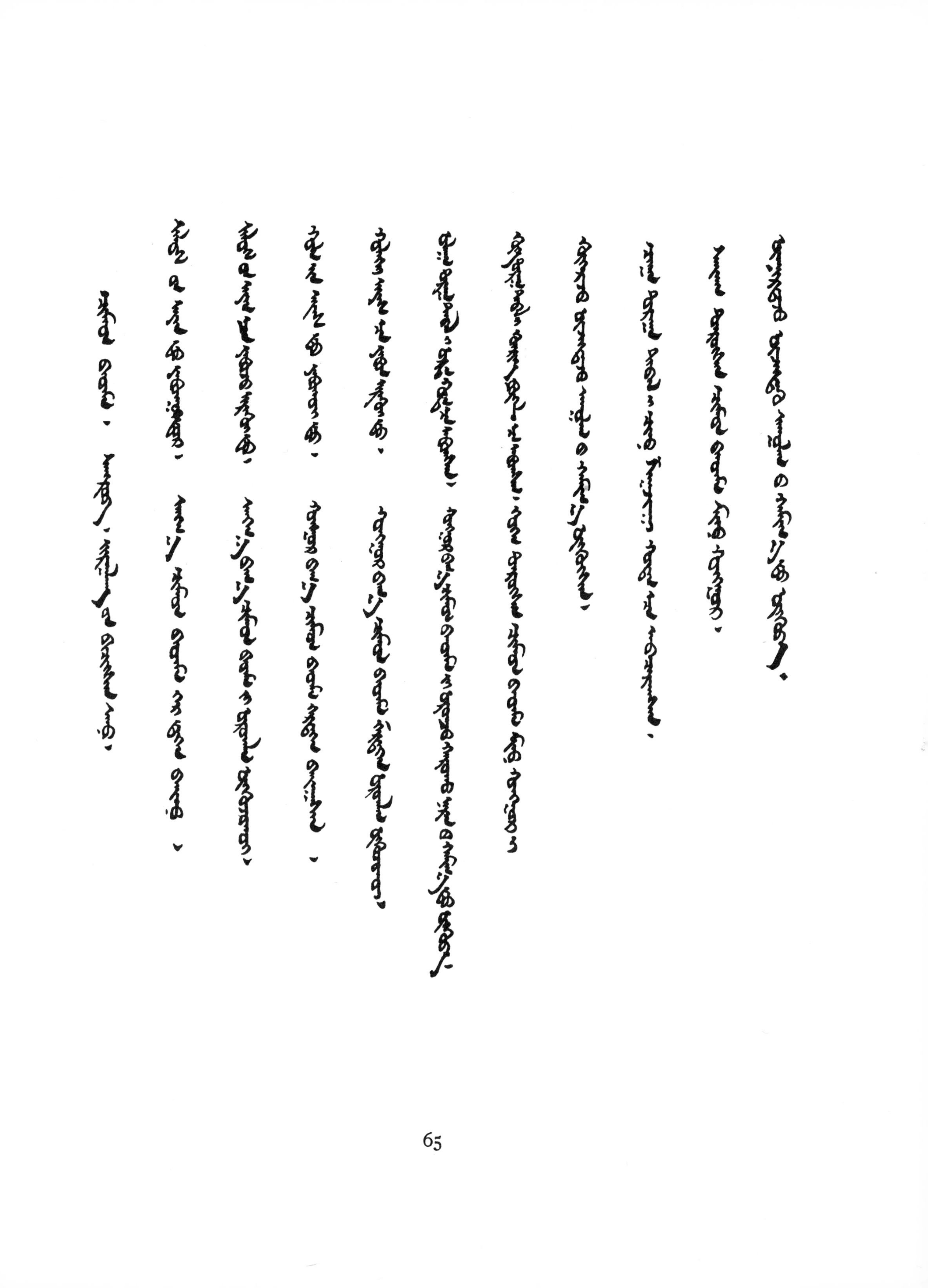

75. THE GREY FROG IN THE WELL.

The grey frog in the well
gets out of the well and cries:
Serneingbo, that son of a thief,
has snatched away his violin and is playing it.

The tadpole in the mud
gets out of the mud and moves about (crying):
Serneingbo, that son of a bitch,
has snatched away his banjo and is playing it.

With a lantern at night-time,
with a watchman at his door,
he feels (as proud) as if he had got the jade seal of the king himself.

With a lantern in the black of the night,
with a soldier at his entrance,
he feels (as proud) as if he had got the jade seal of the emperor himself.

[illegible]
[illegible]
[illegible]
[illegible]
[illegible]
[illegible]
[illegible]
[illegible]
[illegible]
[illegible]
[illegible]

PRELIMINARY REMARKS ON MONGOLIAN MUSIC AND INSTRUMENTS

BY

ERNST EMSHEIMER

The musical material contained in this volume has been transcribed from gramophone-records taken by HENNING HASLUND-CRISTENSEN during his stay in Hsingan-Mongolia in the years 1936—1937.

It is not the aim of the present paper to treat in detail the peculiarities characterizing these melodies or, for that matter, Mongol music in general. Such treatment is reserved for a monograph that will appear later. The following pages will be restricted to the exposition of such elementary data as may be necessary for an understanding and appreciation of the published musical text.

Several publications like the present have already seen the light. In fact, it may be said that the musical genius of the Mongols, as compared with that of other peoples of Inner and Central Asia, has relatively often and early occupied the focus of attention. The first transcription of a Mongol melody was made about two hundred years ago by the Tübingen scholar JOHANN GEORG GMELIN, who took part in the years 1735—45 in the first expedition to Siberia of the then recently founded Russian Academy of Sciences.[1] His example has since been followed by several travellers and explorers; and the fairly comprehensive material that is now available for western research affords an insight into the musical production of a whole series of Mongol tribes.[2]

[1] This transcription was published in Gmelin's account of his journey, Reise durch Sibirien, Part Three, Göttingen 1752, p. 370.

[2] In his book "Melodii mongolskikh plemen" (Zapiski Imp. Russ. Obshchestva po otd. etnografii, Vol. XXXIV, pp. 395 et seq.) the well-known Russian Mongolist A. D. RUDNEV has collected not only the notes made by himself and by friends, but also the entire stock of Mongol melodies that had appeared in print up to the year 1909 (altogether no fewer than 121 melodies). To this publication RUDNEV appended a bibliographical index, that was later published in German translation in the essay by the Finnish scholar ILM. KROHN under the title of "Mongolische Melodien" (Zeitschrift für Musikwissenschaft, 3rd annual number, Leipzig 1920, pp. 65 et seq.). Of the subsequent publications and works containing Mongol melodies the following should especially be mentioned: P. J. VAN OOST, "La musique chez les Mongols des Urdus" (Anthropos, Vols. X to XI, 1915—1916, pp. 358 et seq.), P. BERLINSKII, "Mongolskij pevec i muzykant Ul'dzui-Lubsan-Khurchi (Moscow 1933), M. TRITUZ, "Khal'mg dun" (Moscow 1934), B. BASHKUEV, "Sbornik buriatmongolskikh pesen" (Moscow 1935), and, finally, a collection of songs recently published in France — "Dix-huit chants et poèmes mongols receuillies par la princesse NIRGIDMA DE TORHOUT et transcrits pa Mme HUMBERT-SAUVAGEOT" (Paris 1937).

Valuable as this material is, however, for our knowledge of the musical folk-lore of the Mongols, it suffers from one serious defect. It consists exclusively of notes that were taken down by ear on the spot, without the aid of any technical method of recording. How this may affect the judgment of the published melodies will be clear to everyone who has concerned himself with the problems here under discussion. It is well-known that in the case of notes taken down by ear a whole series of factors enter that make a faithful and objective rendering of the songs a much more difficult matter. This holds especially for melodies with complicated rhythms or tunes. And where several instruments are played together and the person entrusted with the recording has to divide his attention between the singing and the instrumental accompaniment, a reliable recording is quite out of the question. The difficulties that of necessity arise in all these cases are scarcely to be overcome. Indeed, they are not to be mastered even when the collector gets the musicians to go through the same melody several times running, to enable him to fill in missing parts or by comparison to check the correctness of his written version; for, as every student of musical folk-lore knows, the singers and instrumentalists are as a rule incapable of rendering a song even twice in exactly the same way. As a natural consequence of the free delivery that is peculiar to a music depending upon oral tradition, every new rendering of a melody generally falls out in a slightly different way. What in view of these circumstances the recorder is in a position to give, even granted the greatest care and skill, is in the majority of cases no more than the combination of several variants into a more or less fictive picture, but never the full and living reality of a song in all its uniqueness and inimitability as it actually sounded. Since, then, H. HASLUND-CHRISTENSEN when collecting melodies in Hsingan-Mongolia had at his disposal a recording apparatus embodying all the technical qualities required for a satisfactory recording, an extremely valuable and concrete material for study and scientific analysis was acquired. There is probably in no scientific archive in Europe or America a counterpart of this collection.[1] It is now possible, thanks to these records, which enable one carefully to listen to and check the actual individual rendering of a song repeatedly and at will, to get to know even the slightest rhythmical and melodic peculiarities of the music and to reproduce these in modern European transcriptions.

The Material. The material of H. HASLUND-CHRISTENSEN's collection comprises 69 double-sided records with altogether 113 items. Six of these items are spoken

[1] It is true that phonographic records of Mongol melodies have been taken. So, for example, the Phonogram Archive of the Academy of Sciences in Vienna has a number of wax records of Mongol music that were taken during the last war by Prof. R. LACH in Russian internment camps for prisoners of war (cf. L. HAJEK, Das Phonogram-Archiv der Akademie der Wissenschaften in Wien, Zeitschrift für vergleichende Musikwissenschaft, 1st annual publication, 1933, p. 16). But especially the Phonogram Archive of the Academy of Sciences in Leningrad has a splendid collection of phonographic records of Mongol music (cf. S. D. MAGID, Spisok sobranij fonogram-arkhiva fol'klornoj sekcii IAEA Akademii Nauk SSSR, Sovjetskij Fol'klor, Nos. 4—5, Moscow-Leningrad 1936, pp. 415 et seq.).

records, and were therefore not included in the present publication, which has no linguistic or phonetic aims. Two further items, being records of the singing of a Japanese Geisha, were also excluded. The same applies to twelve other items, splendidly successful and from the musical point of view extremely suggestive records of lamaistic cult-music from the monastery Wang-yin Sume. They constitute a permanent record both of the delivery of liturgic cult-texts and of the playing of a temple-orchestra. The reason for their exclusion is not only that lamaist music falls essentially and stylistically outside the scope of Mongol folk-music proper, from which it is strictly differentiated, but also that some peculiarities of lamaist music make it uncommonly difficult, indeed, practically impossible to reproduce it in transcription. The cult-texts are for the most part delivered recitatively, i. e. they are recited by a choir, consisting of lama priests and temple-servants, with a rhythmically stringent scansion either at the same pitch throughout or two neighbouring pitches. The interval between these two pitches, however, is extremely variable and not rationally established. It amounts to approximately a half tone. But apart from this variable interval, also the absolute pitch of these two recitative notes is found to vary. The choir begins on a deep note in the bass register, rising with each repetition of the rhythmical basic formula a step upwards, a step that in its turn is not governed by any definite tone-relation. When the choir has in this way reached the upper limits of its vocal register it sinks back into the bass without transition, to begin again the slow, more or less "chromatically" climbing recitation of the cult-text. It will at once be obvious to the reader that this extreme lability of the tone-relations renders a melodic transcription of the cult-songs impossible. The same applies to the lamaist orchestral music, which consists, if we abstract from its symbolic significance and consider it from a purely musical point of view, of a more or less chaotic medley of sounds. In the recitation of the lamaistic cult-texts it was above all the reproduction of the constant rhythmical basic formula that engaged our attention; in the orchestral music, on the other hand, interest was concentrated rather on the acoustic-effect as such, the naked sound, serving apotropeic aims. Certain absolute pitches or melodic sequences, however, are not intentional. For this reason, also here, a melodic transcription would have been neither possible nor, if it could be achieved, significant. It is scarcely necessary to add that the records of lamaistic cult-music taken by H. Haslund-Christensen in the monastery Wang-yin Sume are none the less in other respects so interesting and noteworthy that it will be necessary to discuss them fully and in detail elsewhere. — Two further records, meantime, that are not here included are the song of a Chipchin Mongol and the flute-playing of a Khorchin Mongol. In both of these cases a transcription was out of the question owing to the extremely uncertain and wavering intonation of the melodies. After the exclusion of all the above-mentioned items, ninety-one items remained for scientific analysis.

By far the greater part of these ninety-one pieces consisted of folk-songs (*duun* or *arat-un daguulal*), in the narrower sense of this term. To this genre must be reckoned also the instrumental melodies, as is apparent from their closed, strophic construction. Only Nos. 33 and 81 seem to constitute an exception, as they apparently belong to a repertoire that is independent of any vocal model, i. e. they are of purely instrumental origin.

It is a characteristic peculiarity of the Mongolian song-genre that, unlike the corresponding musical production of the Turkish nomads of Central Asia, who are both culturally and ethnically related to the Mongols, it is generally not connected by the text or the occasion of its performance to particular seasonal and kalendar events or to special sex or age-groups. True, one does meet with songs in isolated cases that in one way or another are connected with definite usages or activities. To such songs belong, for example, airs that are sometimes played on the eve of a wedding, at a feast, during games or, as with the West Mongols and in part also the Buriats, during the dance. However, the number of such airs is in comparison with the number of songs that are unconnected with any special occasion extremely small. To this category, meantime, must also be reckoned a few songs that, as H. HASLUND-CHRISTENSEN was informed by a Khalkha Mongol, occupy a niche of their own in the general song-repertoire. According to the account of this Mongol it is characteristic of these songs that they are sung only on special and solemn occasions, as for example during the great obo celebrations, during the marriage ceremony etc. They fall, according to their subject-matter, into two groups, namely, 1. *shabrae duun,* or songs with spiritual or didactic import treating of the Buddhist monasteries, the holy lamas etc., and 2. *aidsam duun,* or songs that according to Mongolian tradition date back to the time of CHINGGIS KHAN, and that for the most part have historical import, as for example tales of notable heroic deeds, or praises of olden times etc. The number of these songs is, however, traditionally limited. Thus, the second group is said to comprise only thirty-four songs, and the first groups no more than twelve. As compared, then, with the immense and bewildering wealth of songs that are otherwise to be found among the Mongols and that in the western parts of Khalkha Mongolia are collectively known as *shasjider duun,* the above two groups weigh very lightly in the balance. Songs belonging to the last-mentioned category (*shasjider duun*) must in these parts of the country never be sung on special and solemn occasions — to do so would expose the singers to the charge of crassly transgressing traditional custom and the canons of common decency. It is interesting to note that B. JA. VLADIMIRTSOV[1] has demonstrated the same difference also for the Oirat tribes of north-western Mongolia, whose pastures are adjacent to western Khalkha-Mongolia. This classification has, however, not as yet been shown to apply for other parts of Mongolia. We must therefore assume that it is valid only for certain localities. If one nevertheless decides to apply it to the

1 Obraztsy mongol'skoi narodnoi slovesnosti, Leningrad 1926, p. V.

material published in this volume, then in H. HASLUND-CHRISTENSEN'S opinion one must classify Nos. 29 and 34 under group 1, Nos. 16 and 37 under group 2, and all the remaining songs under group 3.

A sub-group in the present collection is formed by Nos. 30, 44, 46, 48, 49, 84, 86, 87 and 88. These are songs with political propagandistic contents, all of very recent origin.[1] Songs of this kind, however, are found not only in Hsingan-Mongolia, but also among the Volga-Kalmucks, in Buriat as well as Khalkha-Mongolia, i. e. in the region of the Mongol People's Republic.[2] Here, though, corresponding to the very different political conditions obtaining, the propagandistic tendency of the songs is of a completely different colour. The musical characteristics, on the other hand, or at least as far as the Buriat and Khalkha-Mongol songs are concerned, are the same. Some of the melodies, in fact, as for example the tunes of Nos. 46, 84 and 86, are sung in both the regions in question, though of course with corresponding differences in the text. — While the Mongols otherwise seldom sing in chorus, this kind of singing is in the case of the propagandistic songs generally the rule. This does not mean, however, that such songs are not occasionally sung as solos (cf. Nos. 30 and 84).

Another category in the musical folk-lore of the Mongols comprises their epic songs (*uliger*). Both as regards their genesis and the principles of musical style that govern their composition, they form a peculiar and extraordinarily interesting group in Mongolian folk-lore. In the present collection they are not represented by a single specimen. This, however, is no accident. Just as among the Kalmucks and the Khalkha-Mongols, so also among the Mongols of Hsingan-Mongolia epic poetry is becoming a thing of the past,[3] and it is probably for this reason that it was not possible to collect any specimens of this kind of song. In No. 8, on the other hand, we have at least one specimen of a third category in this rich folk-lore in the record of a shamanist song (*duudalga*).

The arrangement of the melodies. The melodies here published have been arranged according to the tribes to which they belong. — In some countries, as for example in Germany, in Finland, and later also in Hungary, the publishers of such collections have tried to arrange the melodies lexically according to purely musical principles. Such methods have both advantages and drawbacks. On the one hand they relieve the reader of a part of the analytical work, and they may thus contribute to facilitate the theoretical study of the material and its assessment for com-

[1] Concerning these songs cf. W. HEISSIG, Der mongolische Kulturwandel in den Hsingan-Provinzen Mandschukuos (Asienberichte, H. 13/14, pp. 70 et seq.).

[2] See M. TRITUZ, op. cit., Nos. 1—12; B. BASHKUEV, op. cit., Nos. 1, 2, 6, 8, 12, 18, 19, 30, 31; P. BERLINSKII, op. cit., Nos. 41—53. Cf. also I. KRAVCHENKO, Fol'klor sovetskoj kalmykii (Sovetskii Fol'klor, No. 6, Moscow-Leningrad 1939, pp. 122—131).

[3] Cf. RYÔ-ICHI-TAKI, The music of the Mongols (Japanese publication), in 'Mongolica', Dec. 1938 (quoted from W. HEISSIG, op. cit., p. 66).

parative investigations. On the other hand, however, lexical points of view entail the risk that those referring to the book may be too much bound by the subjective attitude of the publisher. For this reason we have preferred not to use a lexical arrangement of the melodies in the present publication. Following the express wishes of the editor, it has rather been my endeavour to present the material in as objective a form as possible, uninfluenced by individual points of view. Since, moreover, as has already been mentioned, the greater part of the material belongs to a single category, the song-genre, that is as a rule not connected with special occasions or activities, it was impossible to arrange the melodies according to categories or particular occasions. All things considered, therefore, the most suitable method of arrangement that offered was an ethnological grouping of the melodies according to the tribes that had produced them.

But even this method proved to have complications of its own. It is, for example, especially important not to take this method of classification to mean that e. g. the placing of a song in the group *Jalait* necessarily signifies that the song in question was sung, on the occasion of its recording, by a Jalait-Mongol. The repertoire especially of the professional or semi-professional Mongol singers generally comprises not only songs of the tribe to which by birth they belong. On their wanderings from place to place, from one tribal territory to another, they learn the songs of the most various tribes and include them in their repertoire. In view of this fact, H. Haslund-Christensen found it advisable, when collecting the material, to ask the performers about the origin of the songs they sang. And it is on the basis of the data thus obtained that the arrangement of the melodies according to tribes has been made in this publication.

Those who refer to this collection will, however, doubtless notice that sometimes one and the same melody appears twice, and this in two different places. A case in point is the melody No. 26 in the group *Jalait,* which also occurs as No. 76 in the group *Kharchin.* This may be explained by the fact that the melody in question was composed at a time when these two tribes still belonged together, forming an ethnical or political unit and leading their nomadic life on common pastures. Such a double occurrence may thus sometimes give us an interesting and important indication of definite historical events. It may even in some cases enable us to determine, at least approximately, the age of the song in question. We must, however, beware of falling into the error of attempting to deduce historical connections every time we find a contradiction regarding the origin of a song. For divergences of the kind just described may be due to quite other factors. So, for example, it is possible that certain songs spread, in the course of time, over several tribal territories as so-called "wandering melodies", without our being able to indicate their origin with certainty owing to the lack of a definite tradition. A further possibility is that in different tribes different texts were sung to one and the same melody, and the different data regarding the origin of the song in question referred not, as one might suppose, to the melody but to the text. And finally, it is of course always possible that contradictions and anomalies may be ascribed to faults of memory, actual errors or confusions on the part of the singer himself.

For a number of songs that were recorded in the towns of Hailar and Hsinking no data as to their origin were forthcoming. These have therefore been placed at the end of the present publication in a special group (group M, 1 and 2).

At the very beginning of the work of transcription it became clear that the melodies collected by H. HASLUND-CHRISTENSEN in Hsingan-Mongolia represented two contrary styles, two completely disparate forms of musical expression. These two forms, to whose occurrence in Mongolian music P. J. VAN OOST has already drawn attention,[1] are found in a great number of Mongol tribes. They differ from each other especially in their respective rhythms. By the side of songs having a relatively simple and easily surveyable rhythmical articulation with predominantly straightforward, strict musical time and regular periods one finds others with a completely amorphous rhythm, that it is consequently quite impossible to fit into any rhythmical schema at all. The rhythmical peculiarity of these songs seems to be conditioned by the way in which the text is sung, the syllables being almost imperceptibly now long drawn out, now shortened. Their lengths are always, as measured against the time-units with which our modern European musical notation reckons, somewhat irregular, so that, as R. LACHMANN[2] in connection with a similar rhythmical anomaly in the Japanese No-song very aptly formulates the matter, "the relative time-values can be only approximately expressed by the numerical system used for the time-values of the musical notation".[3] As a rule, both the forms of rhythmical style just described run parallel with corresponding differences as regards the style of delivery and the singing-technique of the singer. Thus, corresponding to the songs with rhythmically clear and well-marked articulation of the musical time, we find a "natural", unforced vocal delivery, whereas in the case of the songs with completely free, irrational musical metre the tone of voice used by the singer is extremely compressed and at the same time very expressive. In the arrangement of the melodies regard was paid to these two categories. Thus, within the main groups classified according to tribes the reader will find first the songs and instrumental melodies with clear and well-marked rhythms, and second those with free rhythms. Of course, this arrangement must not be taken to mean that the former represent a more primitive and in the history of culture older type, while the latter belong to a more differentiated and culturally younger class. As a matter of fact we have every reason to assume the contrary.

[1] Op. cit., pp. 364 et seq.

[2] Musik des Orients, Breslau 1929, p. 65.

[3] The transcription of these melodies was therefore, as regards the rhythm and the tempo, a matter of the greatest difficulty, and must be considered as more or less hypothetical. The metronome indications given here reproduce the tempo of the actual songs only approximatively, and they have been placed, accordingly, in round brackets.

A few songs occupy in point of rhythm an intermediate position between these two styles, e. g. Nos. 2, 7, 16, 38, 58, 68, 70 and 71. It is characteristic of these songs that the salient points in their melodic movement are comparatively speaking clearly marked. Their time, however, changes continually, so that it is not possible to range them in more regularly timed groups. They have thus been included with the category of songs with free rhythm or that with clearly marked rhythm according as typographic convenience was best served.

No further sub-division of the melodies was attempted. The numerical sequence was in other respects dictated by the desire to achieve as practical and from the point of view of handy reference as clear a typographical arrangement of the melodies as possible.

The method of publication. The musical and poetical production of the Mongols depends, as is the case with the musical culture of most non-European peoples and also with European folk-music, on oral tradition. It thus leaves the executants a fairly wide scope for a more or less freely improvising rendering. Their songs do not exist in a form that is in all details permanently established. On the contrary, in the mouth of the singer or under the hand of the instrumentalist they tend, according to the inspiration of the moment, to be rendered always with some slight variation. Each repetition of a melody, even when sung or played by the same singer or instrumentalist several times running, may thus be slightly different. These changes, referred to in the scientific literature of the subject as variants, are for a theoretical investigation of the greatest interest and importance. A comparison of several such variants enables us to decide as to what, in a particular melody, is in tonal and structural respects essential and what is unessential; and the greater the number of variants to be compared, the greater the prospect of attaining reliable results. For this reason, the principle followed in the present publication has been to give as complete a transcription of the melodies as possible, and instead of merely one strophe of a song to give all the strophes occurring in a record.[1]

There were, certainly, some groups of songs where a transcription of all the strophes would have been nonsensical. Such were above all the songs in which the variation, if indeed one may speak of a variation at all in this connection, was restricted, under the influence of the metrical relations of the text, to a rhythmical turning of longer notes into shorter ones or, on the other hand, the exchange of shorter time-values for longer ones. In such cases we have in general contented ourselves with the publication of a single strophe. The same applies for the songs

[1] By "strophe" I mean all the melodies consisting of one or more phrases. In this connection it is a matter of indifference whether such a strophe is rendered by a singer, i. e. with text, or purely instrumentally, either as introductory or concluding accompaniment or else as a kind of ritornello. The strophes are indicated consistently throughout with Roman numerals before the score.

with rhythmically free rendering. It is extremely characteristic of these songs that their strophes show a remarkable melodic conformity, not only as regards the melodic movement as a whole, but also concerning the flourishes and grace-notes that embellish the melodic line, and that in the most striking way repeatedly make their stereotyped reappearance at the same places in the strophe. The changes here take the form of almost imperceptible variations in the rhythmical course of the melody that, as has already been remarked (cf. p. 75, note 3), practically defy all attempts to reproduce them adequately in transcription. In order, however, to give at least a rough idea of these rhythmical variations, we have in a few very marked cases (Nos. 3, 4, 39, 40 etc.) reproduced several strophes. In all other cases we have contented ourselves with the publication of a single strophe.

Where one strophe only has been published we have as a rule given the first strophe. If there were special reasons for giving another strophe this has been indicated by a Roman numeral before the line in question. In some songs, indeed, more marked melodic variants appeared, but their number was too small to justify a publication of all the strophes. For this reason such variants have been given in a special auxiliary score either above or below the standard version, or else they have been introduced directly in the text in the form of auxiliary notes. — In other songs, again, there were strophes that did not, on the whole, differ essentially from the first; while in yet other strophes several notable variations appeared. In such cases we have published, besides the first strophe, also a second or third in extenso.

Where several or all the strophes in a song have been published, these have been arranged in the form of a "comparative score", i. e. corresponding bars, or, where no bar-division was possible, the corresponding periods of the melodic flow have been placed one below the other. The intention has here been to give those using the publication as convenient a survey as possible of the variants, in order thus to facilitate their study. For the same reason, too, the strophes were not written out in full. According to a method of publication used for the first time, as far as I know, by E. v. Hornbostel,[1] only those parts were reproduced that deviated from the first strophe. A certain exception from this rule is constituted by a number of songs that have a purely instrumental introduction. These instrumental introductions consist for the most part of one or two strophes of the song in question. In all these cases we have published in full not only the instrumental introduction, i. e., according to our system of notation, the 1st or 2nd strophes, but in case of need also the third strophe, in order from the example of at least one strophe to illustrate the full, actual harmonic effect produced by all those participating (cf., for example, No. 18).

In applying the principle described for the reproduction of variants a complication arose, and this in connection not only with the songs with instrumental accom-

[1] Ch'ao-t'ien-tze, Eine chinesische Notation und ihre Ausführungen. (Archiv für Musikwissenschaft, 11th year of publication, 1919, pp. 485 et seq.)

paniment, but also with the purely instrumental ones performed with several different instruments. A singer, as we know, generally renders a melody in a different way than for example a flautist,[1] and the rendering of a melody by the flautist differs, in its turn, in melodic and rhythmic respects, necessarily from that of one playing a guitar, a fiddle or a zither, on account of the peculiarities, both technical and acoustic, of his instrument. It would thus have been an error in method to arrange the melodies in such a way that all the variants were referred exclusively to a single line in the score, for example, the first line of the item in question, independently of whether this line represented the melody as rendered by a singer, a flautist, or the player of a guitar or a zither. Obviously, the only right way to introduce the variants in the "comparative score" was to arrange them so that all the variants contributed to the various strophes of a song by, for example, a guitar-player should be referred to the *first* performance of the melody by this instrumentalist, and that correspondingly, all variants contributed by a fiddler or a singer should be referred to the *first* rendering of the melody by the fiddler or singer respectively. In this way all the melodies for fiddle, guitar or flute in a particular song form independent and closed systems of reference that, if they are to be compared, are not therefore necessarily to be immediately coordinated. This method of arrangement doubtless makes things more difficult for the reader. It seemed, nevertheless, advisable to adopt it for the sake of the great advantages of the method for theoretical study.

A further complication arose in connection with a few songs comprising a great number of strophes, the reproduction of which required several pages. A comparison of the different variants with the melodies to which they were referred would here have necessitated a troublesome turning back of pages, that would have interfered with the study of the song. In order to avoid this, the reference-melodies in the songs in question have been re-introduced on the appropriate pages in a special auxiliary score (cf., for example, p. 32 of the musical score).

Just as the comparative investigation of the different variants of a melody is of the greatest theoretical interest, so also, of course, is the case with a comparison of the various melodies with one another. This allows one to study the tonal relations, the different possibilities of melodic conception etc. In order to facilitate this study and to enable the user of this publication to make observations of this kind as quickly as possible, all the melodies here recorded have been transposed in such a way that they can be noted by means of a single scale without any signs before it. Since most of the melodies here published, as is the case with the greater part of all

[1] True, one does often find in oriental music cases where the delivery of a singer is to a great extent influenced by a highly developed and brilliant instrumental technique. (Cf., for example, the record of a song from India, contained in the series of records "Musik des Orients" (No. 17) published by E. v. HORNBOSTEL). As I was able to note from a hearing of the Russian recording of a Buriatic song, Mongol music sometimes shows evidence of a similar influence. In our collection, however, there is no record illustrating the point.

Mongol music, are built up of the notes in a five-note scale without half tones in the same way as for example with Chinese music, and thus belong to the so-called ansemitonic pentatonic scale, the scale of c-d-f-g-a-c' was in general sufficient for their reproduction. Only in the case of a few songs whose melodic construction depended on the combination of two pentatonic scales was it necessary to employ other notes. The same applies, of course, to the numerous cases where extra notes in the form of for the most part unstressed grace-notes, accidentals or passing-notes had to be included.

Naturally, the transposition of all the melodies to a single scale signifies a certain levelling or "standardizing". It takes away a peculiarity that is characteristic for the rendering of the songs, thus robbing them of something of their "individuality". In order to counteract this tendency, the original first note has been indicated by a letter in round brackets at the beginning of each song. The distance between this letter and the first note in the actual score thus represents the interval through which the melodies must be transposed if they are to be reconstructed at their original pitch.

In other respects the notation of the melodies here published follows, on the whole, the principles worked out by O. Abraham and E. v. Hornbostel[1] in the year 1909, which in the course of the last decades have attained universal validity. In some cases, however, owing to a number of peculiarities that are characteristic for the vocal-delivery of the Mongols, it proved necessary to coin and add new diacritical signs. The following table explains their significance:

inverted mordent or mordent occurring not at the beginning of a tone but during the course of its time-value. The auxiliary note is here more strongly accentuated than the principal note.

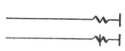

inverted mordent or mordent that occurs immediately at the end of the time-value of a tone. It occurs especially frequently at the conclusion of a melodic phrase.

characteristic breaking off of a tone in singing by one or two sharply expelled breaths. This peculiarity is generally connected with a crescendo-like increase of volume by the singer.

inverted mordent-like shading off of a tone.

a gliding from one pitch to another. The initial tone is in this connection held for the greater part of its time-value, and only immediately at the conclusion thereof does it merge into the next tone glissando.

[1] Vorschläge für die Transkription exotischer Melodien (Sammelbände der Internationalen Musikgesellschaft, 11th year of publication, Berlin 1909, pp. 1—25).

Besides these diacritical signs the following signs and abbreviations were used in the score:

[?]	indicates that the corresponding passage in the record did not come out clearly and could therefore not be transcribed. In the majority of such cases the reason was that the part in question was smothered by other parts.

v.	abbreviation	for	"voice"
fid.	"	"	"fiddle"
gt.	"	"	"guitar"
zt.	"	"	"zither"
fl.	"	"	"flute".

Remarks on the song-texts. It was unfortunately not possible to print the separate parts of the text below the corresponding parts of the score. True, while collecting the songs in Hsingan-Mongolia H. HASLUND-CHRISTENSEN had the texts of many of them dictated by the singers immediately after the recording to a Mongol who was able to write them down. In this way a fine and very valuable collection of song-texts was brought together, that it would have been very desirable to use in the present publication. For only the simultaneous publication of melody and text enables one to judge what extent the construction of the melody from the points of view of form, motif and rhythm has been influenced by the form, the verse-metre or the contents of the corresponding text. And it is only thus that one can get an insight into the structural relations existing between melody and text. It is, however, a circumstance that has already been frequently observed that the texts taken down from dictation differ considerably from the singers' own versions when actually singing the songs. The reason for this divergence between the dictated text and the text as sung is to be found in the fact that melody and text become fused, during the actual singing, to form an indissoluble unit. In the consciousness of the singer they are one and the same. The artificial splitting that inevitably takes place when the singer begins to dictate the text he has just sung creates a psychological situtation that to a not inconsiderable extent affects all the elements in the text-formation. The result is that the texts taken down from dictation show a different composition from that of the texts that have been sung just before. It is therefore only in exceptional cases that the dictated texts enable one to publish below the separate notes of a melody the syllables, words and phrases belonging to them.[1] W. UNKRIG had, indeed, the great kindness to attempt, together with the writer, to fit the texts to the corresponding line with the help of the dictated texts. But for the reasons already given all our endeavours in this direction proved vain. — Attempts to wrest the texts as sung from a hearing of the records, without the help of the corresponding dictated text, also gave, despite the excellent sound-recording of H. HASLUND-CHRISTENSEN'S records, no result. It is, however, well known that in the mouth of a singer the articulation of the words of the text is strongly modified; syllables are long drawn-out, and in some cases phrases and words are to such an extent split, stretched out and extended by the insertion of particles, interjections etc.[2] that their interpretation becomes a problem that without a reliable written text under the melody is scarcely to be resolved even by one having a good knowledge of the language. The melodies published in this volume must thus appear without any underlying texts. The circumstance is to be regretted and constitutes a defect, but a defect that it was impossible to avoid.

The texts collected by H. HASLUND-CHRISTENSEN are by the wish of the publisher of this series to be made available in a special volume. In order, however, to give those using the present publication an idea of the subjects of these melodies, some of the song-texts in the translation of K. GRØNBECH have been included.

Description of the musical instruments. In the following will be given a description of the musical instruments that in one way or another, whether as solo, accompanying or ensemble instruments, were employed in the performance of the melodies collected by H. HASLUND-CHRISTENSEN in Hsingan-Mongolia. The instruments in question are four in number, and in this publication they are referred to as "fiddle", "zither", "guitar" and "flute". They may on the whole be said to comprise the complete list of instruments used by the Mongols of to-day — if we except the numerous instruments employed in the lamaist divine service.[3] In their construction these four instruments appear as typical products of the nomadic way of life. They are comparatively simply made; they are handy; they are easily carried by their owners on their wanderings over the steppe; and finally, being the reverse of blaring or noisy, they are well adapted for a small audience. Instruments of percussion are as little found among the Mongols as among the Turkish nomads of Central

1 The procuring of the texts is, as everyone who has had anything to do with the collection of musical material in the field well knows, without doubt one of the most complicated aspects of the work of music-collecting. In my opinion the only way of obtaining the adequate song-text is to have it taken down during the actual singing by an educated and well-versed native.

2 A. D. RUDNEV draws attention to this phenomenon in his article "Ein mongolisches liebeslied" (Journal de la Société Finno-Ougrienne, XXIII, 18, p. 4). He writes: "Der Mongole geht sehr willkürlich mit dem texte um und schiebt viele unnütze silben ein, nur um den text der musik anzupassen."

3 Concerning the use of the jew's harp by the Mongols cf. my essay "Ueber das Vorkommen und die Anwendungsart der Maultrommel in Sibirien und Zentralasien" (Ethnos, Vol. VI, Nos. 3—4, pp. 117 et seq.).

Asia with whom they are related, except for the shamanic drum, which, however, occurs in a special connection, for which reason it will not here be discussed.

Of the four Mongolian instruments mentioned, that which is most deeply rooted in the musical life of the people is undoubtedly the *fiddle*. Two characteristic types of this instrument are met with.

The first of these is of special interest. It consists of a trapezoid sound-box, through which a wooden stick is thrust. Two strings of horse-hair are fastened to the stick where this emerges at the bottom and drawn taut over the sound-box by means of lateral pegs (see pls. II, III, 1—2, IV, VII, 1—2, 4, VIII, 1). This kind of fiddle is found, besides in Mongolia and occasionally in China, only in North Africa.[1] It is possible that it was also known to the Arabs in pre-Islamic times.[2] The occurrence of such a characteristic instrument in two places so comparatively remote from each other is striking. Whether this coincidence is to be explained in the light of a historical connection, and whether we have here perhaps to do with an interesting parallel in the domain of musical instruments to the relations that E. v. HORNBOSTEL and R. LACHMANN[3] believed themselves to have traced in the domain of music between East Asia and North Africa must be left for a special investigation to decide.

The name given to this type of instrument by the different tribes in Mongolia varies somewhat. Thus, H. HASLUND-CHRISTENSEN notes among the Sunit Mongols the term *khil-khuur* (in the written language: *kili kugur*). In Khalka Mongolia, on the other hand, the instrument is called simply *khil*,[4] while the Buriat Mongols refer to it as *khur*.[5] The latter designation occurs, says H. HASLUND-CHRISTENSEN, not only among the Buriats but also among the Khorchin Mongols.

The construction of this kind of fiddle varies. As the instrument has been hitherto very little discussed in the literature dealing with musical instruments, we will describe its constituent parts in some detail in the following.[6] Our description is based upon seven specimens of the instrument, taken from different parts of Mongolia. Four of these specimens (St. 1—4) are preserved in the collections of The Ethnographical Museum of Sweden in Stockholm,[7] one (H. 1) is privately owned

1 See G. A. VILLOTEAU, Description historique, technique et littéraire des Instruments de Musique des Orientaux, in Description de l'Egypte, Paris 1823, p. 353.

2 See H. G. FARMER, Article 'Rabab' in 'Enzyklopädie des Islams', Vol. III, p. 1172.

3 Asiatische Parallelen zur Berbermusik (Zeitschrift für vergleichende Musikwissenschaft, Vol. I, Berlin 1933, pp. 4 et seq.).

4 See P. BERLINSKII, op. cit., p. 41.

5 See I. RYK, Narodny muzykal'nye instrumenty Buriat-Mongolii (Isskustvo Buriat-Mongol'skoi ASSR, Moskva-Leningrad 1940, p. 82).

6 The designations of the separate parts of the instrument have been taken from a glossary compiled by H. HASLUND-CHRISTENSEN and K. GRØNBECH among the Sunit-Mongols and kindly placed at my disposal.

7 Museum Nos. and origins of the instruments:
St. 1: 29, 21. 94 — Dzakchin Mongols.
St. 2: H. 2577 — Edsen-gol Mongols.
St. 3: H. 30 — Chakhar Mongols.
St. 4: H. 2627 — Edsen-gol Mongols.

by H. HASLUND-CHRISTENSEN,[1] while the other two (K. 1—2) were acquired by H. HASLUND-CHRISTENSEN during his last expeditions in southern Mongolia for the National Museum in Copenhagen.[2]

The most important part of the instrument in the eyes of the Mongols is obviously the sound-box. This seems evident from its designation: *tologhä* (written *tologaj*), i. e., literally, "main" in the meaning of "main part". Its construction is rather primitive. Four laths of wood are joined together to form a trapezoid frame, whose lower area is as a rule greater than the upper area. Only among the Manchu Mongols, as H. HASLUND-CHRISTENSEN was able to observe, is the opposite relation between the areas the rule. Here the smaller area of the frame is turned downwards, so that the sound-box does not, as in the case of the other instruments, taper upwards, i. e. towards the neck, but broadens (see pl. II, 1; VII, 2). It is interesting to note that the corresponding Chinese instrument, of which A. C. MOULE[3] gives an illustration under the designation *ta-hu-ch'in,* has the same construction. It is possible that this agreement is to be explained by the fact that the Manchu Mongols are descended from Chinese "slaves" who in the 18th century arrived in Khorchin Mongolia in the suite of a Manchu princess, and there married Khorchin Mongol women.[4]

No definite rules seem to exist for the proportions of the frame. These vary, at all events, not inconsiderably. Measurements carried out on six of the instruments at our disposal gave the following results, expressed in centimeters:[5]

	St. 1	*St. 2*	*St. 3*	*H. 1*	*K. 1*	*K. 2*
Lower area:	27.1	20.9	28.5	23.3	19	19.1
Upper area:	17.2	17	17.3	16.6	16	26
Height:	37	22.5	30.7	24.5	20.5	29
Depth:	10.6	4.6	6.3	6.7	7.7	7.7

When the frame is finished, the front and back are covered with hide (*äris,* written: *arisun* = hide) that has been freed of hair. Only the Manchu Mongols seem also in this respect to proceed in a slightly different manner than the other tribes. Some tufts of hair that were left on the ribs of the instrument acquired by H. HASLUND-CHRISTENSEN among the Manchu Mongols evidently indicate that the hair was removed from the hide after this had been stretched onto the frame (see pl. VII, 2.). — This latter operation is carried out as follows: the hide is stretched on the

[1] Origin of the instrument: Chakhar Mongols.

[2] Museum Nos. of the instruments: K. 1: Collection HASLUND-CHRISTENSEN, No. 18/39, R. 833 — Chakhar Mongols. K. 2.: 18/37, R 127 — Manchu-Mongols.

[3] Chinese Musical Instruments (Journal of the Royal Asiatic Society, Vol. XXXIX, 1908, pl. VI).

[4] Cf. O. LATTIMORE, The Mongols of Manchuria, London, 1934, pp. 229 et seq.

[5] The measurement of the Copenhagen instruments was kindly performed by H. HASLUND-CHRISTENSEN.

Fig. 1. Sound-holes of a *khil-khuur*.

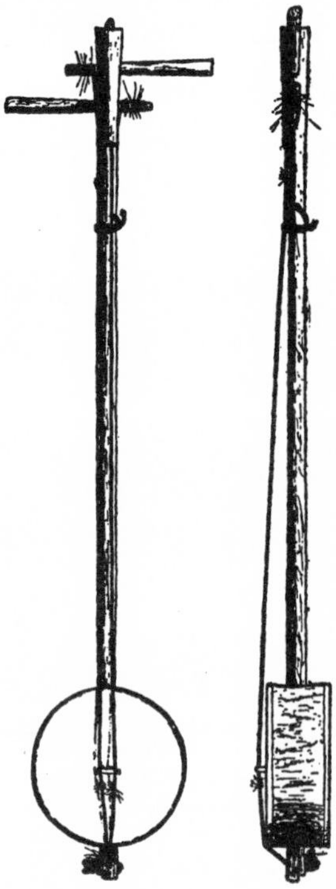

Fig. 2. Drawing of a *khil-khuur* with circular body from the Edsen-gol. The Ethnographical Museum of Sweden, Stockholm (Mus. No.: H. 2627). Cf. Pl. IV.

sound-box front and back, and either glued, nailed, or even sewn to the ribs thereof. In the case of an instrument coming from the Edsen-gol (St. 2), however, the process was somewhat different. A single piece of hide was here wrapped round the wooden frame in such a way that both front and back were completely covered, as well as the ribs.

Sometimes, instead of animal hide, some other material is used to form the front and back sides of the sound-box. So, for instance, the constructor of the fiddle belonging to the Dzakchin Mongols nailed a piece of thin brass-plate to the front side of the sounding-box (see pl. VII, 4); and for the back of the Chakhar Mongol instrument preserved in Copenhagen wood was used.

The significance attached by the Mongols to the sound-box is evident from the pains and care often expended on the artistic shaping thereof. Front and back, as well as the ribs, are painted and in some cases richly ornamented. In fact, in the case of the Chakhar-Mongol instrument, an unusually magnificent specimen, the sides and the wooden back have even been ornamented with elaborate carvings, representing, besides purely ornamental figures, also animals (see pl. VII, 1). The sound-holes, too, on the back of the instrument, are treated with especial care. They are always circular in form, and by means of segment-like formations they are shaped into an artistic ornament (see fig. 1).

Among some Mongol tribes, particularly, it would seem, among Torgut tribes, the trapezoidal sound-box is sometimes replaced by a circular body. An illustration of this form is provided by an instrument (St. 4) acquired in the Edsen-gol oasis by Dr G. MONTELL during the Hedin-Bendix Expedition in the year 1930 (se fig. 2; pl. IV). The diameter of the body of this instrument is 16 cm, its depth is 6.2 cm.[1]

The next step after completion and covering of the frame is, as has already been mentioned, the thrusting of a wooden stick (*ish,* written *eshi* = handle, stem) longitudinally through the sound-box. This stick serves to bear the strings. Its length seems to be as little laid down in any definite rule as the proportions of the sound-

[1] A. Kalmuck fiddle of the same type, though with strings of gut instead of horse-hair is described by B. BERGMANN (Nomadische Streifereien unter den Kalmüken in den Jahren 1802 und 1803, 2. Theil, Riga 1804, p. 173) under the name *dombur*. Besides this instrument the Kalmucks also use another two-stringed fiddle, obviously borrowed from the Qazaqs (see fig. 4 A).

box. In any case, it varies not a little, as may be seen from the following measurements:

St. 1	*St. 2*	*St. 3*	*St. 4*	*H. 1*	*K. 1*	*K. 2*
105	109.4	113.4	83.8	103.5	110.2	96.5

The wooden stick often ends in an ornamental elaboration representing the head of a horse (see pl. III, 1). The occurrence of this sort of ornament is in my opinion not accidental. One finds similar plastic representations also on the handles of staffs used by the Mongol shamans in the performance of their rites. This agreement seems to indicate that the Mongol fiddles were at one time shaman instruments, and originally, in the same way as the shaman staffs and the shaman drums, represented the mythical riding animals upon which, as the Mongols imagine, the shamans rise on their journeys into the realm of spirits.

When the wooden stick has been fastened to the sound-box, two strings are attached and drawn taut. The material for these is provided by strands of black or, though apparently more seldom, white horse-hair. The deeper string is called by the Mongols *budung utas* (written *budugun utasun* = thick string), and the higher one *närin utas* (written *narin utasun* = thin string). Before these two strings are drawn taut, however, some firmer material is knotted to their two ends — a piece of plaited horse-hair, a leather cord or even simply a silken or hempen cord. The idea of this is doubtless to replace the more sensitive horse-hair at those places where the technical demands upon its powers of resistance are greatest with some suppler and more resistant material.

The fastening of the strings at the top, to the neck of the instrument, is compassed with the help of wooden pegs called *chikhe* (written *chikin* = ear). This designation seems to indicate that the Mongols regard or have at one time regarded the instrument as an animate being. This also speaks in favour of the supposition that the fiddles originally served the Mongol shamans as a part of their magical paraphernalia.

The strings are fastened to the pegs, as may be seen from the instruments at our disposal, in different ways. What appears to be relatively the most primitive method — a method, moreover, that occurs in south-east Celebes and in the Spice Islands[1] — is that according to which the strings are affixed to the pegs not in the middle but at the side of the neck of the instrument. In this case two holes must be bored diagonally in the neck, in order to bring the strings forward from the side, i. e. towards the middle of the neck (see fig. 2). Another and more differentiated procedure, that more nearly approaches the construction of the European instrument, entails hollowing out a broad groove in the stick at the top, where the strings, at their

[1] Cf. C. Sachs, Die Musikinstrumente Indiens und Indonesiens, 2nd edit., Berlin and Leipzig 1923, p. 109.

attachment to the pegs, end. This groove may be made on the front or also on the back side of the neck. In the latter case, however, two small holes must be bored right through the neck, through which the strings are then drawn from the back to the front (see pl. II, 2). And finally, a third method of fastening the strings to the pegs is clearly traceable to Chinese models. According to this method a separate peg-box is made and then mortised into the neck in such a way as to incline slightly backwards (see pl. VII, 2, 4).

From the pegs, the strings are drawn under a loop of string (*darabch,* written *darubchi* = that which presses). This string fits tightly around the neck of the instrument, and in such a way that it may be pushed within certain limits either upwards or downwards. This enables the player of the fiddle to raise or lower the pitch of his instrument at will, and thus to adapt it to the pitch of his voice. The same function is served, moreover, by a small movable bridge (*bagha dewkhe,* written *baga tebke* = little bridge) that in some instruments is affixed to the neck immediately below the string-loop (see pl. VII, 1).[1] The two strings are then drawn down from above over the bridge proper (*yikhe dewkhe,* written *yeke tebke* = big bridge). This bridge is situated about in the middle of the sound-box and marks the lower limit of the vibrating part of the string. According to a Khalkha-Mongol tradition,[2] this bridge is supposed to be made out of the inferior jaw-bone of a human being. This is thought to enable the player of the instrument to "sing" with especial expressiveness. Unfortunately, we have no information as to whether this tradition obtains also in other parts of Mongolia. The instruments themselves seem to contradict this assumption, for the bridges of all the fiddles at our disposal are made of wood, not of bone.

Immediately below the bridge the two strings are knotted to the already mentioned more resistant material. By means of this latter, referred to as *senj* (written *senji* = button-hole, or ear), the strings are fastened below to the stick protruding from the sound-box.

The instrument is played with a more or less curved bow of reed or of wood (*datuur,* written *tatagur* = that with which one plays) that is loosely strung with horsehair. According to Khalkha-Mongol tradition, this hair must be taken from the tail of the horse.[3] It is not, however, sufficient that the hair should be taken from the tail of any horse. Thus, the greatest preference is shown for the tail of an exhausted horse. Only on this condition is it possible for the player to give expression with the bow to all his joy and sorrow. — Before the actual playing begins, as H. Haslund-Christensen observed among the Sunit-Mongols, the bow-string is thoroughly

[1] This bridge is present in only two of the instruments at our disposal (K. 1 and H. 1). Whether it was originally affixed to the other specimens or not I could not determine.

[2] See P. Berlinskii, op. cit., p. 15.

[3] ibidem.

rubbed with pulverized rosin (*shen-shan-kin),* that is generally procured from Chinese merchants.

The tuning of the two strings of the instrument always occurs in fifths. But the absolute pitch of the open strings varies according to the construction and size of the instrument. Moreover, as has already been remarked, the pitch of one and the same instrument may within certain limits be altered by means of the string-loop and the little movable bridge. The range of this variation amounts, as practical experiments have shown, to about a fifth. Sometimes, too, a piece of wood is also used, being wedged more or less firmly under the strings, between the bridge and the string-holder (see pl. VIII, 1). The tension of the strings is thus more or less increased, whereby the absolute pitch of the instrument is made still higher or deeper.

Finally, attention may be drawn to an original method of changing the timbre of the instrument that H. Haslund-Christensen observed among the Sunit-Mongols. This method consists in sticking a knife under the bridge of the fiddle (see pl. III, 2). As a result, the vibration of the tones is considerably intensified. According to H. Haslund-Christensen, the effect thus produced is extremely popular among the Sunit-Mongols.

During the actual playing the instrumentalist kneels on the ground. He supports the instrument on the ground with his left hand between his thighs, allowing it to rest lightly against his left thigh with the deep string towards him (see pl. II, 1—2). With his right hand he manipulates the bow. The tension of the bow-string is regulated during play with the little finger.

The manipulation of the instrument evidently varies. So, for example, I. Ryk[1] writes that among the Buriat-Mongols only two fingers are used to produce the different tones on both strings. In this case it is clear that melodies with a wide range will necessitate a continual change in the position of the player's hand. H. Haslund-Christensen, on the other hand, informs us that the Sunit-Mongolian fiddlers use all five fingers of the left hand in playing. Only the four fingers, however, are used for the notes required on the high string, while the less frequently recurring notes of the deep string are taken with the thumb. The method of producing the different notes is everywhere the same. The strings are not pressed firmly against the neck of the instrument; instead, the notes are produced in a more flute-like manner, i. e. by means of a light pressure with the tip of the finger. The timbre of the instrument by no means reminds one, however, of the flute-like notes of our modern European stringed instruments. The tones produced are relatively powerful, and remind one of the timbre of the human voice more than do those of our European violins.

As has already been stated above, one finds in Mongolia, besides the type of fiddle

[1] Op. cit., p. 82.

just described, also another type. — Among the Sunit-Mongols it bears, according to H. HASLUND-CHRISTENSEN, the name *dörwen chikhe khuur* (= four-eared *khuur*). The Khorchin-Mongols, on the other hand, have the designation *khorae,* and the Khalkha-Mongols *khuur* or *khuuchir,* the latter term referring to a smaller sub-type.[1] The term *khuuchir* is also current among the Buriat-Mongols for this type of instrument,[2] as is also the term *khor.*[3] Among the Kalmucks it is called a *biwa,* a term that seems to be etymologically related to the designation *p'i-p'a* for the Chinese pear-shaped lute.

The points in which this type of instrument differs from the one we have just described refer especially to the form of the sound-box and the number of the strings. The sound-box is not trapezoid, nor even circular; it is cylindrical in shape (see pl. V, 1), or, though more seldom, it forms a hexagonal or octagonal prism of wood (see pl. VII, 3). As a rule, the front side is covered with hide. Instead of the two horse-hair strings, four strings of silk are used. Here, too, however, the instrument is tuned in fifths, and in such a way that the strings harmonize in pairs. The strings are not, as in the previous type, fastened to the neck of the instrument by means of lateral pegs, but by means of front or rear pegs. No string-loop or small movable bridge is here employed. Instead of these devices we find a movable metal ring loosely attached by means of a loop to the neck of the instrument, and through this ring the strings are drawn. When the player moves this ring upwards or downwards the length of the vibrating part of the four strings is automatically shortened or lengthened, and the pitch of the instrument correspondingly altered. Also in this case the instrumentalist plays in the crouching position; though here, instead of balancing his instrument on the ground he supports it lightly on his left thigh (see pl. V, 1). The bow-string is manipulated with the right hand. In contradistinction to the manner of manipulating the bow-string employed in the case of the two-stringed fiddle, however, the bow is here, as with the Chinese fiddle, drawn between the strings in two strands, and in such a way that the player is the whole time touching either of the two pairs of harmonizing strings. The bow-string is thus permanently attached to the instrument.

The manner of producing the notes is the same as that employed with the previous type, i. e., the notes are produced in a flute-like manner; the player touches the strings with the end-joints or the middle joints of the four fingers. As H. HASLUND-CHRISTENSEN informs us, the notes on this instrument are sometimes produced by touching the strings from below with the surface of the finger-nails.

The origin of this type of instrument is as yet rather obscure. According to Chinese tradition it originated in the north, i. e. in present-day Mongolia. In how far one is justified in assuming this type of instrument to be Mongolian in origin

[1] See P. BERLINSKII, op. cit., p. 41.
[2] See I. RYK, op. cit., pp. 82 et seq.
[3] See JOH. GOTTL. GEORGI, Beschreibung aller Nationen des Russischen Reichs, St. Petersburg 1776, p. 431.

must be left an open question. All that we actually know is that fiddles were first imported to China in the period of the T'ang dynasty (618—907), and that thereafter, thanks to the powerful impetus everywhere developed by Chinese culture, they spread over the whole of East Asia and beyond.

Most closely akin to the Mongolian four-stringed fiddle is the Chinese *su-hu*.[1] The agreement between these two instruments is in respect of the construction almost complete. They differ only in point of size, the Mongolian fiddle being considerably bigger than the Chinese *su-hu;* when played, it generally out-tops the head of the player by several hand-breadths. In order to give some idea of the proportions of the instrument, we give here below the measurements of a Chakhar-Mongol fiddle that H. HASLUND-CHRISTENSEN acquired for the National Museum in Copenhagen[2] (see pl. VII, 3):

Length of neck:	90.8 cm
Length of body:	18.7 cm
Outer diameter of body:	12.5 and 10.5 cm
Inner diameter of body:	10 and 9.4 cm

H. HASLUND-CHRISTENSEN also draws attention to the fact that the sound-colouring of the Mongolian fiddle is always darker, softer and less sharp than that of the Chinese *su-hu*. He tells us also that for this reason the Mongol musicians prefer to make their fiddles themselves, rather than buy Chinese models from merchants.

Both the fiddle-types described, the four-stringed and the two-stringed, are intended in the first place as instruments for accompaniment. Less frequently they may also be used as solo instruments. In this case, however, the melodies played upon them are for the most part variations on melodies that are known in vocal form. Two items of this kind are represented in the present publication (Nos. 37 and 80). In all the other cases (Nos. 17—21, 50—53, 72—73, 76—78) the fiddle serves the singers as accompanying instrument. Unfortunately, it was not possible to ascertain on which of the two fiddle-types the accompaniment was played in particular cases. There are no data on this point; and neither an analysis of the timbres of the respective instruments nor an examination of the bowing technique and the pitches occurring gave, when listening to the records, any evidence from which reliable conclusions might have been drawn.

[1] Concerning the construction of the *su-hu* cf. MOULE, op. cit., p. 127, and M. COURANT, Essai historique sur la musique classique des Chinois (Encyclopédie de la musique, ed. A. Lavignac, I., Paris 1913, p. 182).

[2] Museum No.: Collection HASLUND-CHRISTENSEN No. 18/39, R. 831.

Another very ancient musical instrument, that seems, however, at present to be falling into disuse, is the Mongolian *zither* (pls. VI, 2; VIII, 2). H. HASLUND-CHRISTENSEN, at least, says that this instrument is to-day very seldom met with in Mongolia and is in any case felt as old-fashioned by the Mongols themselves. P. BERLINSKII,[1] too, states that there is only one old man left in Khalkha-Mongolia who knows how to play the zither. The explanation given by P. BERLINSKII for the disappearance of this instrument from Mongolia is interesting. According to his account, which agrees, on the whole, with the observations made by H. HASLUND-CHRISTENSEN, the zither is in the first place a court instrument, and it has of all Mongolian instruments the most complicated and difficult technique. Its mastery thus calls for a comparatively intensive specialization and long and regular practice on the part of the instrumentalist. These requirements, however, are on account of the revolution in the economic and social conditions that has of recent years taken place in Mongolia increasingly difficult of fulfilment. The political and economic power of the Mongolian feudal princes is so much on the wane that the court-musician is more and more deprived of the material basis of his existence. This, then, is why the number of Mongolian zither-players continues steadily to decrease, while their tradition is gradually being lost and even the instrument itself tends to disappear. We have thus the greater cause to rejoice that H. HASLUND-CHRISTENSEN succeeded, more or less at the eleventh hour, in recording and saving for the future some really expertly rendered zither-items in Hsingan-Mongolia (cf. especially Nos. 90 and 91).

The names by which the zither is known to the Mongols vary but little, and the slight differences they may show are purely dialectal. In western and Khalkha-Mongolia and among the Volga Kalmucks[2] it is called *jatag* or *jataga*,[3] in Chakhar-Mongolia, on the other hand, the instrument is named *itag* or *jitag*. A slightly different sounding designation, *yaduga,* by which we have proof that this instrument was known also in Central Asia and Persia at the court of the Mogul rulers in the 15th century,[4] is noted by P. J. VAN OOST,[5] as well as in the dictionary compiled by I. E. KOWALEWSKI.[6]

The instrument itself belongs to the group of zithers with open strings, i. e. the notes are not here produced, as in the case of the Chinese *ch'in,* by pressing the

[1] Op. cit., p. 13.

[2] See N. A. NEFEDEV, Podobnyja svedenija c volzhskich kalmykakh (Zhurnal' ministerstva vnutrennikh del', ch. XIII, St. Petersburg 1834, p. 226).

[3] Also the Orenburg Qazaqs call their zithers by this name, cf. A. L. MASLOV, Illiustrirovannoe opisanie muzykal'nykh instrumentov, khraniashchikhsia v dashkovskom etnograficheskom muzee v Moskve (Izv. Imp. Obshchestva liubitelei estestvoznaniia antropologii i etnografii, Vol. CXIV, Moscow 1911, p. 215).

[4] Cf. H. G. FARMER, Reciprocal Influences in Music 'twixt the Far and Middle East (The Journal of the Royal Asiatic Society, 1934, pp. 339 et seq.).

[5] Op. cit., p. 395.

[6] Dictionnaire mongol-russe-français, Kazan 1844—49.

fingers on different parts of the strings, but simply by plucking the unmodified strings. The mode of playing is thus the same as that employed with the Chinese *cheng,* with which it is closely related. Here, too, a long, rectangular box of wood is made, with the cover slightly arched and the lower end forming an obtuse angle. As a rule, twelve strings of spun silk are stretched over this sound-box. Among the Volga Kalmucks, it is true, one finds the instrument in a more primitive form, with seven or eight strings of brass or gut.[1] On account of the far-reaching agreement between the Mongolian zither and the Chinese *cheng* it often happens that Mongolian zither-players use Chinese instruments instead of those manufactured by themselves (cf. pl. III, 2).

Despite the close relationship existing between the Mongolian zither and the Chinese *cheng* as regards their construction, there are, nevertheless, one or two characteristic peculiarities that at once enable one to distinguish the two instruments. These differences are apparent even to a superficial glance. Thus, the Mongolian zither is notably richer and more individual in design than the relatively simple and unpretentious Chinese *cheng.* The Mongol instruments are painted in gay colours and embellished with ornaments. Especially characteristic in this respect is a specimen acquired in 1938/39 in Chakhar-Mongolia by H. HASLUND-CHRISTENSEN. This instrument, preserved in the National Museum in Copenhagen,[2] besides being very artistically painted, is richly provided with carvings (see pl. VI, 2). But there are differences not only in the matter of ornamentation, but also in point of construction. In particular, the Mongol way of attaching the strings to the instrument is evidently different, as a rule, from that employed by the Chinese. While the strings of the Chinese *cheng* are always drawn through on the back side of the instrument, those of the Mongolian zither are knotted to little metal rings at the end on both sides just immediately below the raised cross-piece (see pl. VIII, 2). The Chákhar-Mongol instrument mentioned above illustrates, it is true, a somewhat different combined procedure. The strings are here knotted to the little metal rings only on one side, while on the other side, on the narrow side of the instrument, they are fastened to metal pegs, as are the strings of the Chinese *la-chʻin.*[3]

It would seem that the proportions and size of the Mongolian zither are as little subject to any definite rules as those of the fiddle. Thus, P. I. VAN OOST[4] gives 160 cm as the total length of the instrument, while the length of the Chakhar-Mongolian instrument in Copenhagen is 114.5 cm and its breadth 21.6 cm. The respective lengths of the straight and the sloping surfaces is here in the ratio of approximately 5 : 1. Another Chakhar-Mongolian zither, on the other hand, preserved in the Ethno-

[1] Cf. N. A. NEFEDEV, op. cit., p. 226, and also G. J. RAMSTEDT, Kalmückisches Wörterbuch, Helsingfors 1935, p. 217 a.

[2] Museum No.: Collection HASLUND-CHRISTENSEN No. 18/39, R. 968.

[3] Cf. A. C. MOULE, op. cit., p. 120.

[4] Op. cit., p. 395.

graphical Museum of Sweden in Stockholm,[1] is 153.4 cm in length and 22 cm in breadth, the respective lengths of the straight and the sloping surfaces being in the ratio of approximately 10:3.

The scale of the Mongolian zither is, like that of the Chinese *cheng,* pentatonic. The instrument thus has a range of slightly more than two octaves. Whereas, however, for the performance of the zither-tunes contained in the present publication the instrument was tuned stepwise, K. GRØNBECH has noted among the Sunit-Mongols the following interesting tuning of the zither:

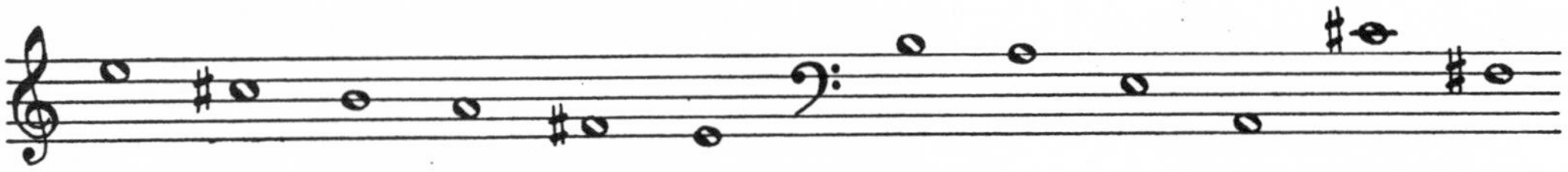

Doubtless the tuning of the instrument in this form was undertaken in order to enable the player conveniently to employ a quint-bourdon.

The tuning of the zither is performed by the Mongols, from the technical point of view, in the same way as that employed by the Chinese for the tuning of their *cheng,* i. e. the player places movable sharp bridges under the strings on the soundbox of the instrument. The position of these single bridges determines the length of the vibrating part of the strings. Apart from these bridges, as has already been observed, the Chakhar-Mongolian instrument in the Copenhagen Museum has on its narrow side small metal pegs by means of which the tension of the strings may be regulated, and that also serve as a tuning arrangement.

The zither is played in the following way: the player kneels on the ground, laying the upper part of the instrument on his thigh and supporting the lower sloping part on the ground. He plucks the strings immediately above the uppermost bridge either directly with the thumb and forefinger or with two plectrums affixed thereto. These plectrums (*khume* = nail) generally consist of leather caps for thumb and finger to which is attached a little piece of horn. The fingers of the left hand are as a rule used to exercise a more or less strong pressure on the strings behind the bridge (see pl. III, 2). Through this pressure the bridge is thrust slightly downwards, the tension of the vibrating part of the strings becomes successively greater and the note that has just been plucked rises glissando.[2] This technique is, however, apparently not obligatory. In the performance of the four zither tunes recorded by H. HASLUND-CHRISTENSEN in Hsingan-Mongolia, in any case, it was not once used. One does, meantime, occasionally meet with another technique (cf., for example, No. 35, bar 8), that consists in setting the string just plucked in vibration with the fingers of the left hand. This method has been briefly described by P. S. PALLAS.[3]

[1] Museum No. H. 29.

[2] The same manner of playing is described as early as in the 15th century by ABD AL-QADIR IBN GHAIBI (d. 1435) in connection with the Chinese *cheng.* See H. G. FARMER, Reciprocal Influences ......, p. 340.

[3] See P. S. PALLAS, Sammlungen historischer Nachrichten über die Mongolischen Völkerschaften, 1st part, Frankfurt and Leipzig 1779, p. 231.

The timbre of the instrument reminds one of the sound of the cembalo. It is generally used as a solo instrument, though there are exceptions to this rule (cf. Nos. 34 and 36).

As we have already remarked, the melodies recorded by H. HASLUND-CHRISTENSEN include, besides those played on fiddles and zithers, some played on the *guitar*. Guitar and lute-like instruments, as far as I have been able to ascertain, occur among the Mongols in three different types.

The first type of guitar in vogue is referred to as a *tobshuur*.[1] It is in shape very reminiscent of the above-described two-stringed fiddle. Here, too, the sound-box is trapezoid and is pierced with a stick to which two strings are attached by means of lateral pegs (see fig. 3). The only point of difference in the construction of the two instruments is in the somewhat more compact form of the *tobshuur*. The sound-box is comparatively broad and the neck correspondingly shorter. Among the Oirats of north-west Mongolia this instrument is extremely popular. VLADIMIRTSOV[2] states that it is the inseparable companion of the Oirat singers of heroic songs, who are unable to render their epics without its accompaniment. Besides among the Mongols it is also found among the Altai tribes and the Uriankhai.

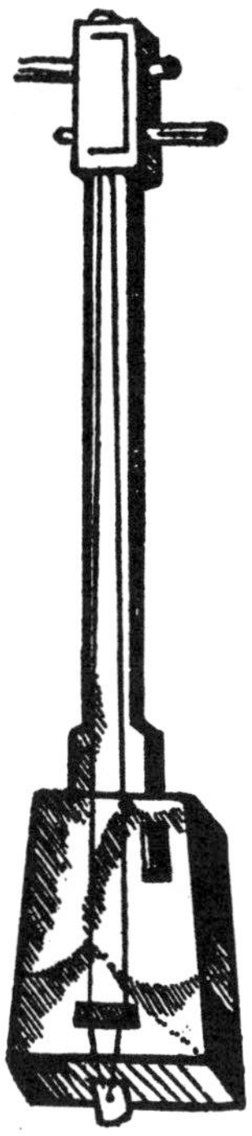

Fig. 3. Mongolian tobshuur. Drawing after Z. V. EVALD, Music and Musical Instruments (Sibirskaya Sovetskaya Enciklopedija, Vol. 3, 1932).

The second type, with its triangular sound-box, its long narrow neck with shiftable frets and two strings, is identical with the Qazaq *dombra* (see fig. 4). As far as I know, we find the type under this name only among the Volga Kalmucks, where it seems to have ousted the type, known as the *tobshuur*, that we have just described.

The third type, known as the *shandze*, corresponds exactly to the Chinese *san-hsien* (see pl. III, 3). It is found especially among those Mongol tribes that are more or less intimately connected with Chinese culture, as for example among the Buriats and the tribes in Khalkha and Hsingan-Mongolia. H. HASLUND-CHRISTENSEN tells us that all the guitar-melodies recorded by him in the field were played on this type of instrument.

The instrument itself has been frequently described in the literature of the subject.[3] It consists of an oval sound-box, covered on both sides with snake-skin. Through this sound-box a stick is thrust, to which above and below three strings of spun silk are attached. No data are available as to how these strings are tuned by the Mongolian guitar-players. Instead of a jade plectrum, as H. HASLUND-CHRISTENSEN observed, the Mongols use a little piece of horn. Sometimes, however, the strings are simply plucked with the fingers. The sound thus produced is very sharp,

[1] B. IA. VLADIMIRTSOV, Mongol-oiratskii geroicheskii epos, Petersburg-Moscow 1923, p. 24.
[2] ibidem, p. 39.
[3] Cf. A. C. MOULE, op. cit., p. 116; and M. COURANT, op. cit., p. 178.

Fig. 4. Interior of a Kalmuck tent, showing a player on the *dombra*. Top-left a Qazaq *kobys*. Top-right a Kalmuck *dörwen-chikhe-khuur*. After P. Pallas.

but quick-fading. The players therefore generally endeavour to pluck any particular note not only once but several times running.

The fourth of the instruments to be discussed is the *flute*. The flutes most commonly met with in Mongolia to-day are transverse flutes of the *ti-tse* type (see pl. V, 2). They are almost unanimously called by the Mongols *limba*.[1] Occasionally, however, one also finds vertical flutes. Thus, P. S. Pallas,[2] for example, gives a very clear description of a primitive Kalmuck vertical flute (*zurr*) with three stops made from the hollow stem of a big "sun-shade plant" (Sonnenschirmpflanze) and allied to the Bashkir *kura* or the Kirghiz *choor*. Also P. I. van Oost[3] mentions the occurrence of a vertical flute. This type, however, is rarely met with. The flute tunes recorded by H. Haslund-Christensen in Hsingan-Mongolia were all performed on the transverse flute of the *ti-tse* type.

1 *Limba,* as W. Unkrig tells me, is a modification of the Tibetan *glin-bu*. The final vowel *u* appears also in the word *limbu,* noted by P. I. van Oost (op. cit., p. 394) among the Ordos Mongols. This word is here used, however, to designate not the transverse flute but the vertical flute. The transverse flute is called a *bishur*.

2 Op. cit., 1st part, pp. 231 et seq. 3 Op. cit., p. 394.

There is no lack of data concerning the construction of the transverse flute of this type,[1] so there is no need in this place to enter into details. As a rule, this flute consists of a tube, open at the bottom end and having twelve stops. The lips of the player are applied to the 1st of these twelve stops; a further hole has a piece of thin paper glued over it, and serves to colour the timbre of the instrument. The six next holes, bored at equal intervals, are for the fingering. And finally, the four remaining holes, two of which are situated on the upper side of the flute while the other two are situated in a parallel position below, are beyond the reach of the fingers and thus do not serve for the production of particular notes. But the player may block them up with any suitable material and thus give the instrument a deeper pitch.

It would of course be an interesting task to try to ascertain to what extent the construction and mode of playing of the four types of instrument described above contributed to the form and manner of the melodies played on them. Such an investigation, however, falls outside the scope of an introduction, and will be undertaken elsewhere in connection with a general critical and analytical study of Mongol music.

In conclusion, it is my pleasant duty to thank all those who have helped me in the preparation of this volume. Especially I am indebted to Dr Sven Hedin, who has from the first shown the greatest interest in my work and supported it in every way. To him, therefore, I wish to tender my warmest thanks. I am equally indebted to H. Haslund-Christensen, who has throughout been a willing source of valuable information. He has been untiring in the communication of the numerous and interesting observations on the musical life of the Mongols that he made during the long period of his meritorious and fruitful work as a collector in Mongolia. The information I have had from him has been for me of the greatest value, and I offer him my most cordial thanks. Further, it was owing to the great kindness of the Stockholm Broadcasting Company that I was permitted to carry out the transcription of the melodies published in this volume in the rooms of the company. A special studio was placed at my disposal for this work; and the excellent technical arrangements that were made available contributed in no small measure to facilitate my work. Moreover, copies of the original gramophone-records were made for me whenever I needed such as working material. I wish to take advantage of this opportunity of tendering my heart-felt gratitude to the management of the broadcasting company for all their kindness, and for the practical help that I received on so many occasions during the course of my work in the studio.

I am also deeply indebted to Dr Gösta Montell for the interest and comradely support he has shown in connection with my work. And finally I wish to thank Mr Donald Burton for his translation of this introduction.

[1] Cf. A. C. Moule, op. cit., pp. 78 et seq. and M. Courant, op. cit., pp. 154 et seq.

Data connected with the single melodies.

Tribe	No. of the melody	No. of the record	No. of strophes recorded	No. of strophes published	REMARKS. The numbers refer to No. of the melody
A. Buriat . .	1	78a	10	1(I)	1 Some west- and Khalkha-Mongolian variants of this melody are given by A. D. RUDNEV (op. cit., p. 01, No. 4 and S. 05, Nos. 26, 26a). Cf. also No. 47 in our collection.
	2	78b	9	9(I—IX)	
B. Chipchin	3	89	10	10(I—X)	
	4	91	7	7(I—VII)	
	5	77	8	1(I)	
	6	76	10	1(I)	
	7	102	21	2(I—II)	7 Strophe II is the melodic and rhythmic basic form of the song, that as opposed to strophe I represents a somewhat more ornamented variant (cf. bars 1 and 3). The singer rises during the rendering of the 21 strophes by about a minor third.
	8	86			
C. Daghur .	9	105	6	6(I—VI)	9 The (female) singer rises from the beginning to the end of the song by something more than a whole tone.
	10	104		1(I)	
D. Ölet . . .	11	97	8	8(I—VIII)	11 Here, too, the intonation rises continually, by about half a tone.
	12	72a	15	12(IV—XV)	12 Strophes I—III are intoned in a hovering and uncertain manner, only from strophe IV onwards is the intonation sufficiently stabilized to allow of transcription.
	13	72b	7	7(I—VII)	
	14	80	10	1(I)	
E. Jalait . . .	15	75	10	2(I—II)	
	16	68	5	5(I—V)	16 = 37. The intonation rises until the end of the song by about half a tone. A variant of this melody written down in Kalgan has been published by A. D. RUDNEV (op. cit., p. 03, No. 16).
	17	96	6	6(I—VI)	17 Before the song begins, the instrument is tuned to the notes c—g. The same tuning applies also for the fiddle melodies of the following numbers.
	18	100	9	9(I—IX)	18 A variant of this melody is given by P. BERLINSKII (op. cit., p. 70, No. 32).
	19	98	6	6(I—VI)	19 = 53.
	20	99	6	6(I—VI)	
	21	101	6	6(I—VI)	
	22	83	13	13(I—XIII)	22 The alternation of flute and song in this item is not common, says H. HASLUND-CHRISTENSEN, in Mongolia. The present example, as also in the following songs (Nos. 23—28), was due to a suggestion by H. HASLUND-CHRISTENSEN. In this group of songs one frequently finds fairly long pauses between the strophes that are sung and those rendered on the flute; these are indicated in the score. As metrically 'dead' pauses they are without musical significance; they indicate the time required by the flautist, who is at the same time a singer, to return the instrument to his lips at the end of the singing.
	23	90	17	17(I—XVII)	
	24	84	8	8(I—VIII)	24 The voice of the singer sinks in the course of a strophe by about half a tone.

Tribe	No. of the melody	No. of the record	No. of strophes recorded	No. of strophes published	REMARKS The numbers refer to No. of the melody
E. Jalait . . .	25	94	13	13(I—XIII)	25 Cf. P. BERLINSKII, op. cit., p. 78, No. 46 and B. BASHKUEV, op. cit., p. 5, No. 1.
	26	85	9	9(I—IX)	26 = 76. A variant of the same melody has been published by P. BERLINSKII (op. cit., p. 71, No. 35) and also by B. BASHKUEV (op. cit., p. 8, No. 8).
	27	92&88	19	19(I—XIX)	
	28	106	11	11(I—XI)	28 = 75; cf. P. BERLINSKII, op. cit., p. 68, No. 27.
F. Khorchin	29	14	7	1(I)	29 Cf. No. 35. This song was accompanied simultaneously on the flute and the fiddle. Both instruments, however, were almost completely drowned by the choir, so that a transcription was not possible.
	30	19	7	1(II)	30 = 34. The beginning of strophe I (bars 1—4) is missing on the record. For this reason strophe II is published here.
	31	13a	4	4(I—IV)	31 This melody was executed by a flautist and a guitar-player together. The latter, however, was evidently not very familiar with the tune, so that owing to his defective performance there are numerous divergences in the respective versions of flute and guitar. We therefore contented ourselves with publishing only the rendering of the flautist. The same applies to the two following items.
	32	13b	4	1(I)	
	33	13c	1	1(I)	
	34	15	6	1(I)	34 This melody was played by a flautist and a fiddler together. The fiddler, however, plays the melody with very indistinct intonation and lags, in his tempo, behind the flautist, so that there is continual rhythmical clashing between the two. Only the flautist's part was, therefore, transcribed.
	35	6	9	9(I—IX)	35 Cf. No. 29. In strophe 5 (7th note) the guitar-player inadvertently intercalates an extra eighth pause, so that in relation to the playing of the zither up to the end of strophe 5 his part is behind by an eighth, though he apparently does not notice this. In the musical score this inadvertency on the part of the guitar-player is corrected, while the guitar-part is given in its original form in a special score under the corresponding line of the transcription. Variants of this melody have been published by B. BASHKUEV (op. cit., p. 15).
	36	7	5	3(I—III)	36 = 72. The departures from the basic melody appearing in the guitar-part must not be understood as genuine variants. Rather are they due to the embarrassment of the player, who is not sufficiently acquainted with the song, and therefore frequently waits until the zither-player has produced the following note in the melody before he can himself play it. His performance is thus very hesitant, and rhythmically unprecise. In many cases he produces a note that is displaced by the time-value of an eighth (see bars 8—14). For the same reason one presumes that in those places in the score that are provided with a question-mark the guitar-part is not covered by that of the zither. The guitar-player here pauses, to see which note he is to produce next.

Tribe	No. of the melody	No. of the record	No. of strophes recorded	No. of strophes published	REMARKS The numbers refer to No. of the melody
F. Khorchin	37	11a			37 = 16.
	38	20	5	5(I—V)	38 = 58.
	39	16b	4	4(I—IV)	39 = 40.
	40	16a	4	4(I—IV)	40 = 39.
F/1 Khorchin Jasaktu	41	42	5	1(III)	41 The record begins in the middle of strophe I (bar 7). By way of conclusion the (female) singer repeats only the first four or eight notes.
	42	45	12	1(I)	42 The singer's intonation rises in the course of the 12 strophes by about half a tone.
	43	21a	7	1(I)	43 The choir is accompanied by 2 flutes and 2 fiddles. These are, however, barely audible, and it was therefore not possible to transcribe them.
	44	21b	8	1(I)	44 The intonation rises in the course of the 8 strophes by about half a tone.
	45	40	6	6(I—VI)	45 In strophe I of this item the (female) singer mixes up two different songs. She begins with one melody (bars 3—9), and from bar 10 onwards continues with another, that is then repeated five times running in its entirety (strophes II—VI). For this reason strophe II was given in the score as reference melody, instead of strophe I.
	46	43a:1	5	1(I)	46 = 84 and 86. Variants of this melody have been published both by P. Berlinskii (op. cit., p. 76, No. 41) and B. Bashkuev (op. cit., p. 35, No. 31).
	47	43a:2	7	2(I—II)	47 The singer here begins his song with the two first bars of melody No. 46 (= Nos. 84 and 86). On bar 3 he goes over to the proper melody, that he then repeats in its entirety six times (strophes II—VII).
	48	65		1(I)	
	49	66	9	1(I)	
	50	29	5	1(I)	50 Presumable tuning of the instrument = c—g, cf. Nos. 17—21.
	51	30	6	6(I—VI)	51 Before this song is begun the instrument is tuned to the notes c—g.
	52	33	7	7(I—VII)	
	53	26	10	10(I—X)	53 = 19. The purely instrumental rendering of the song on the fiddle and the guitar serves here as introduction (strophe I). In the following, however, the fiddle-part is submerged by the singer's voice. It was thus not possible to transcribe the fiddle-part in strophes II—X.
	54	17	4	1(I)	
	55	18	7	1(I)	
	56	23	6	2(I—II)	
	57	24	9	1(I)	
	58	27	2	2(I—II)	58 = 38.
	59	28	6	2(I—II)	
	60	31	10	1(I)	
	61	32	5	1(I)	61 Strophes I—III of this song are sung by a woman; strophes IV—V, on the other hand, by children.
	62	34	7	1(II)	62 The record begins in the middle of strophe I; strophe II was therefore published here instead.
	63	35	7	1(I)	
	64	37	4	1(I)	

Tribe	No. of the melody	No. of the record	No. of strophes recorded	No. of strophes published	REMARKS The numbers refer to No. of the melody
F/1 Khor-chin Jasaktu	65	38	5	1 (II)	
	66	41	8	1 (III)	
	67	43b	5	1 (I)	
	68	44	6	3 (I, III, V)	
	69	48	10	2 (I—II)	
	70	49	5	4 (II—V)	70 The record begins at the end of strophe I.
	71	50	5	5 (I—V)	
G. Gorlos . .	72	3	8	8 (I—VIII)	72 = 36. This item consists of an alternation of a purely instrumental rendering (strophes I, II, V, VII) and an instrumentally accompanied vocal rendering of the melody (strophes II, IV, VI, VIII). Since, apart from a few insignificant divergences, the singer does not vary the melody, the score includes, for strophes IV, VI and VIII, only the parts of the two accompanying fiddles.
H. Tumet . .	73	36	6	1 (I)	
I. Barin . . .	74	39	5	1 (I)	
K. Kharchin	75	5	7	7 (I—VII)	75 = 28.
	76	1	5	5 (I—V)	76 = 26.
	77	25	6	6 (I—VI)	
L. Chakhar .	78	8	7	7 (I—VII)	78 What has been said above concerning No. 72 applies also to this item. The vocal part was therefore not transcribed for strophes IV and VI.
	79	12c	2	2 (I—II)	
	80	12a	5	1 (I)	80 Before the item is begun the instrument is tuned to the notes C sharp — G sharp.
	81	12b	—	—	
M/1 Hailar .	82	70	7	7 (I—VII)	
	83	71	21	1 (I)	
	84	74a	4	4 (I—IV)	84 = 46 and 86.
	85	73	13	6 (I—VI)	
	86	74b	5	1 (I)	86 = 46 and 84.
	87	95a	8	1 (I)	87 Cf. P. Berlinskii (op. cit., p. 49, No. 47).
	88	95b	3	1 (I)	
M/2 Hsinking	89	2	3	3 (I—III)	
	90	10	3	3 (I—III)	90 = 91.
	91	9	3	3 (I—III)	91 = 90.

Alphabetical list of the singers and the melodies sung by the same, where the names are known.

Achingan	No. 74	Jimbil	No. 83
Bilgündalei	Nos. 17—21	Maksar	Nos. 43, 54—55
Buyantoktakhu	No. 12	Öljeitoktakhu	Nos. 15, 22—28, 84
Chin yü	No. 90	Sangrub	Nos. 38, 46, 57, 62, 67, 70—71
Golimbuu	Nos. 3—6, 14, 82, 85	Semen	Nos. 61, 65
Hiou Shung-en	No. 53	Temürbagan	No. 77
Hu Yung-tai	No. 30	Tseridar	No. 7

List of the melodies.

Vocal: Nos. 1—16, 29—30, 38—39, 41—49, 54—71, 74, 82—88

Songs with instrumental accompaniment:

with fiddle: Nos. 17—21, 50—52, 72—73
„ „ & guitar: Nos. 53, 76—78
„ flute: Nos. 22—28
„ „ & guitar: No. 75
„ zither & guitar: Nos. 35—36

Instrumental:

Fiddle: Nos. 37, 80
Guitar: No. 81
Zither: No. 90
„ & guitar: No. 91
Flute: Nos. 31—34, 40, 79, 89

H. Haslund—Christensen with the recording apparatus that was used for the recording of the melodies given in Collection 2. Photo: J. v. Utfall.

Pl. II.

1. Manchu Mongol playing the *khil-khuur*. This instrument is preserved in the National Museum, Copenhagen (cf. Pl. VII, 2). Photo H. Haslund—Christensen.

2. Chakhar Mongol plays a song about horses to his horse on a *khil-khuur*. This instrument is preserved in the National Museum, Copenhagen (cf. Pl. VII, 1). Photo H. Haslund—Christensen.

1. Sunit Mongol playing the *khil-khuur*. Photo K. GRØNBECH.

2. The same *khil-khuur,* lower half. In front a *yatag*. Photo K. GRØNBECH.

3. *Limba*-player from Sunit. On the ground a *shandze*. Photo K. GRØNBECH.

Pl. IV.

Edsen-gol Mongol playing *khil-khuur* with circular body. This instrument is preserved in the Ethnographical Museum of Sweden, Stockholm. (Cf. p. 84, fig. 2). Photo G. Montell.

1. Mongol playing the *dörwen-chikhe-khuur*. Photo G. Montell.

2. *Limba*-player. Photo K. Grønbech.

1. Impoverished Mongol troubadour of the old school with his most precious possession, the *dörwen-chikhe-khuur,* that he carries on his back. Photo H. Haslund—Christensen.

2. *Yatag* from Chakhar Mongolia, richly decorated with Buddhist motifs and symbolic figures. Cf. p. 37, fig. 2. Preserved in the National Museum, Copenhagen (Museum No.: Collection Haslund—Christensen, No. 18/39, R. 968). The instrument was manufactured about 1860 by a celebrated instrument-maker. Photo H. Haslund—Christensen.

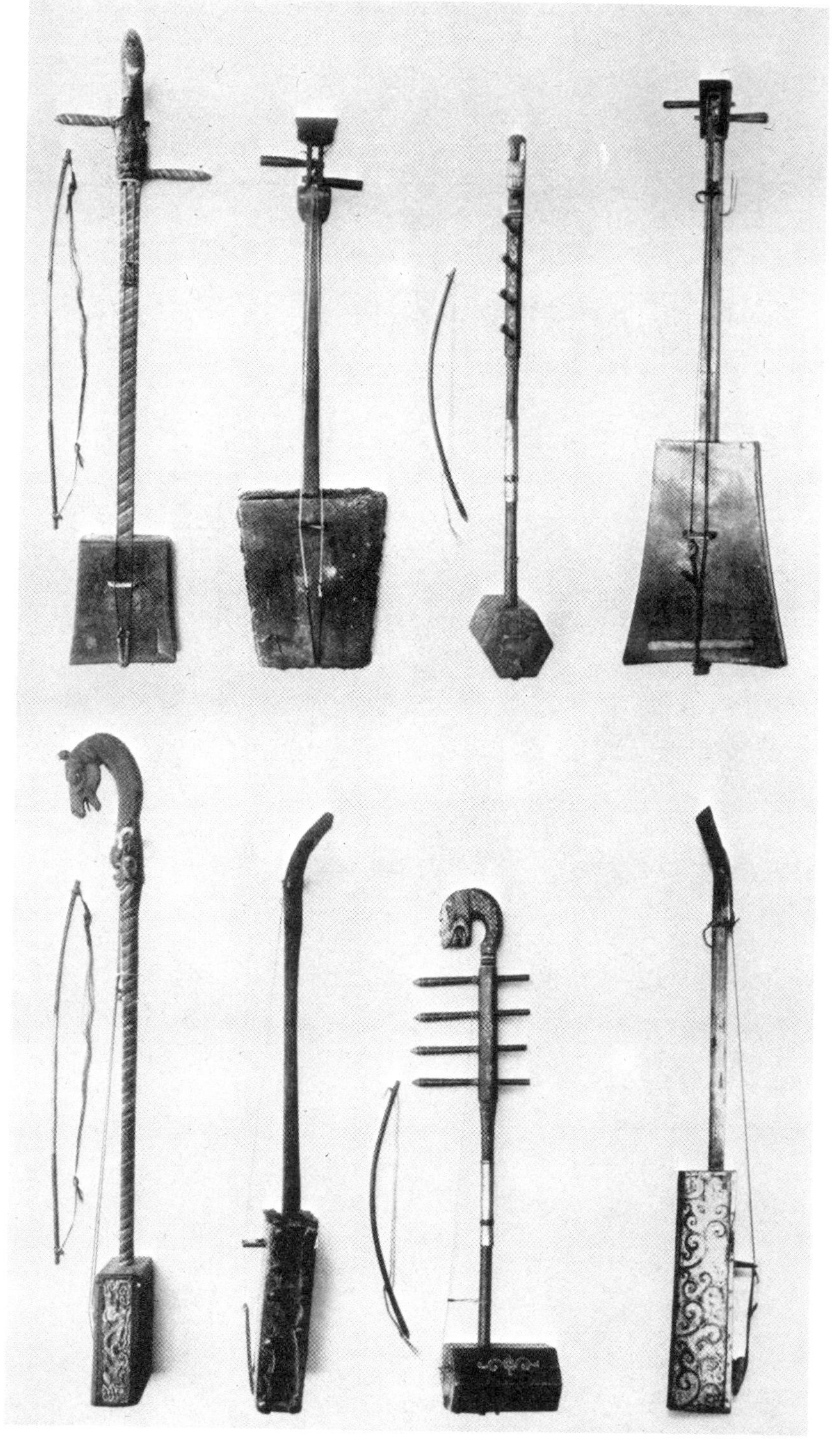

Fiddles collected by H. Haslund—Christensen in various parts of Mongolia:

1. *Khil-khuur* from Chakhar. The National Museum, Copenhagen (Mus. No.: Collection Haslund—Christensen, No. 18/39, R. 833),
2. *Khil-khuur* from the Manchu Mongols. The National Museum, Copenhagen (Mus. No.: Collection Haslund—Christensen, No. 18/37, R. 127),
3. *Dörwen-chikhe-khuur* from the Chakhar Mongols. The National Museum, Copenhagen (Mus. No.: Collection Haslund—Christensen No. 18/38 R. 831),
4. *Khil-khuur* from the Dzakchin Mongols. The Ethnographical Museum of Sweden, Stockholm (Mus. No.: 29, 21. 94). Photo G. Nykvist.

Pl. VIII.

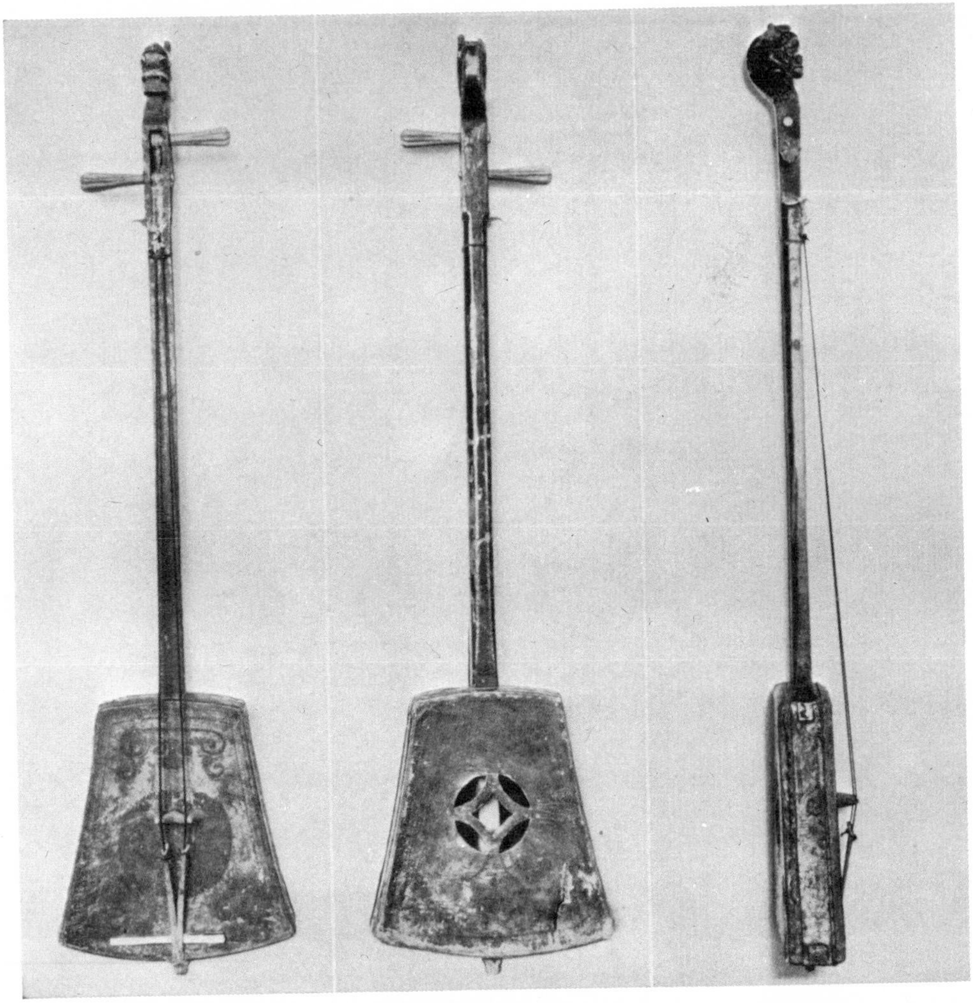

1. *Khil-khuur* from the Chakhar Mongols. The Ethnographical Museum of Sweden, Stockholm (Mus. No.: H. 30). Photo G. NYKVIST,

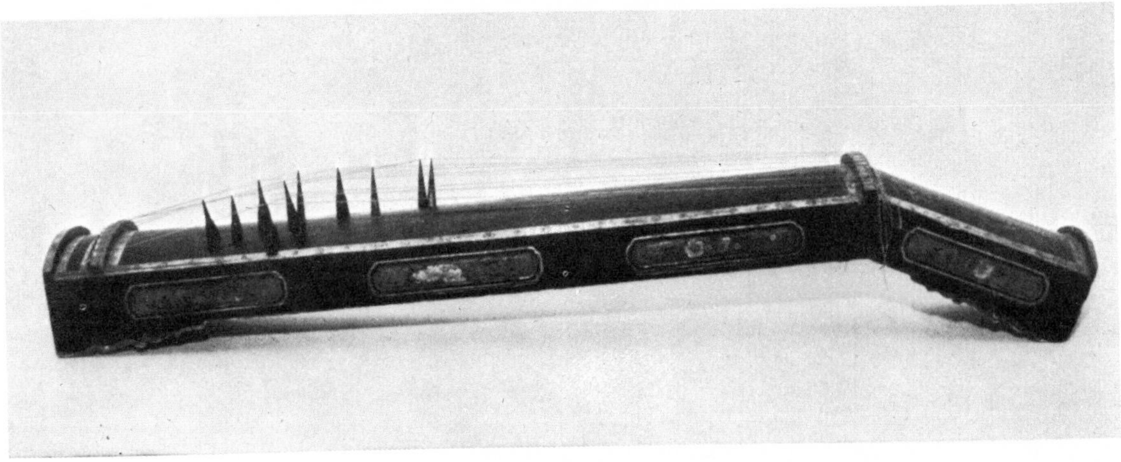

2. *Yatag* from the Chakhar Mongols. The Ethnographical Museum of Sweden, Stockholm (Mus. No.: H. 29). Photo G. NYKVIST.

MUSIC OF EASTERN MONGOLIA

collected by

H. HASLUND-CHRISTENSEN

noted down by

ERNST EMSHEIMER

BURIAT

Degedü monggol-un khaguchin dagu

Old song of the famous Mongols

Male voice (b♭) ♪ = 120—126

Male voice (f) ♩ = 92

B

CHIPCHIN

3 Tus jirgal agula

The mountain Tus Jirgal

4 Umakhai Khabung-un dagu

The song of Umakhai Khabung

Male voice (g)

♩ = (92)

5 Bogdo agula-yin barga

Bargas of the Holy Mountain

6 Urtu saikhan

Long and beautiful

7 Kürdün chagan chilagu

The round white stone

Obo-u onggo-yin oriksan

Prayer to the spirit of the obo

C

DAGHUR

9

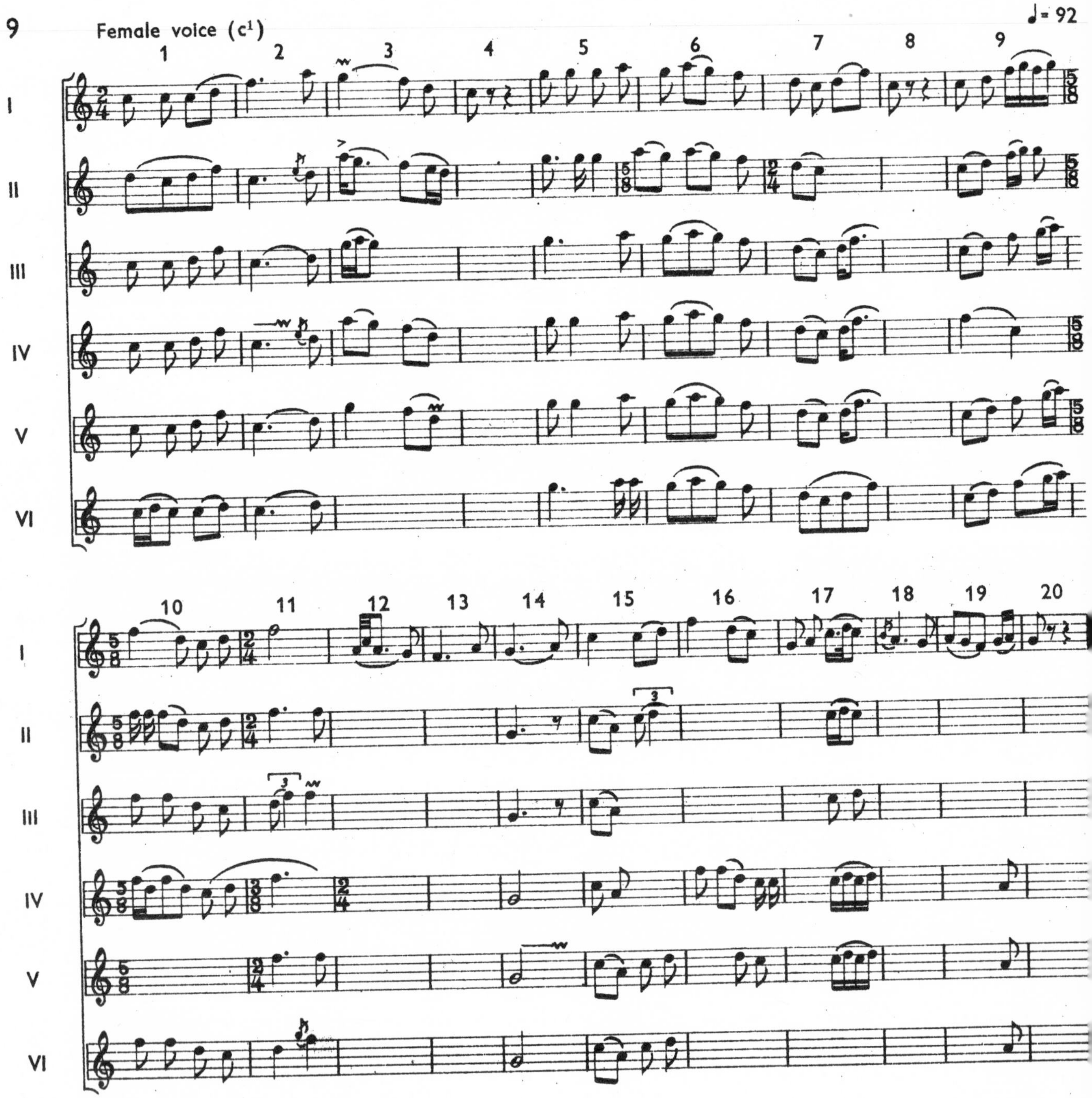

10

D

ÖLÖT

11 *Soldiers' song*

Male voice (c#)

♩= 92 acc. to 138

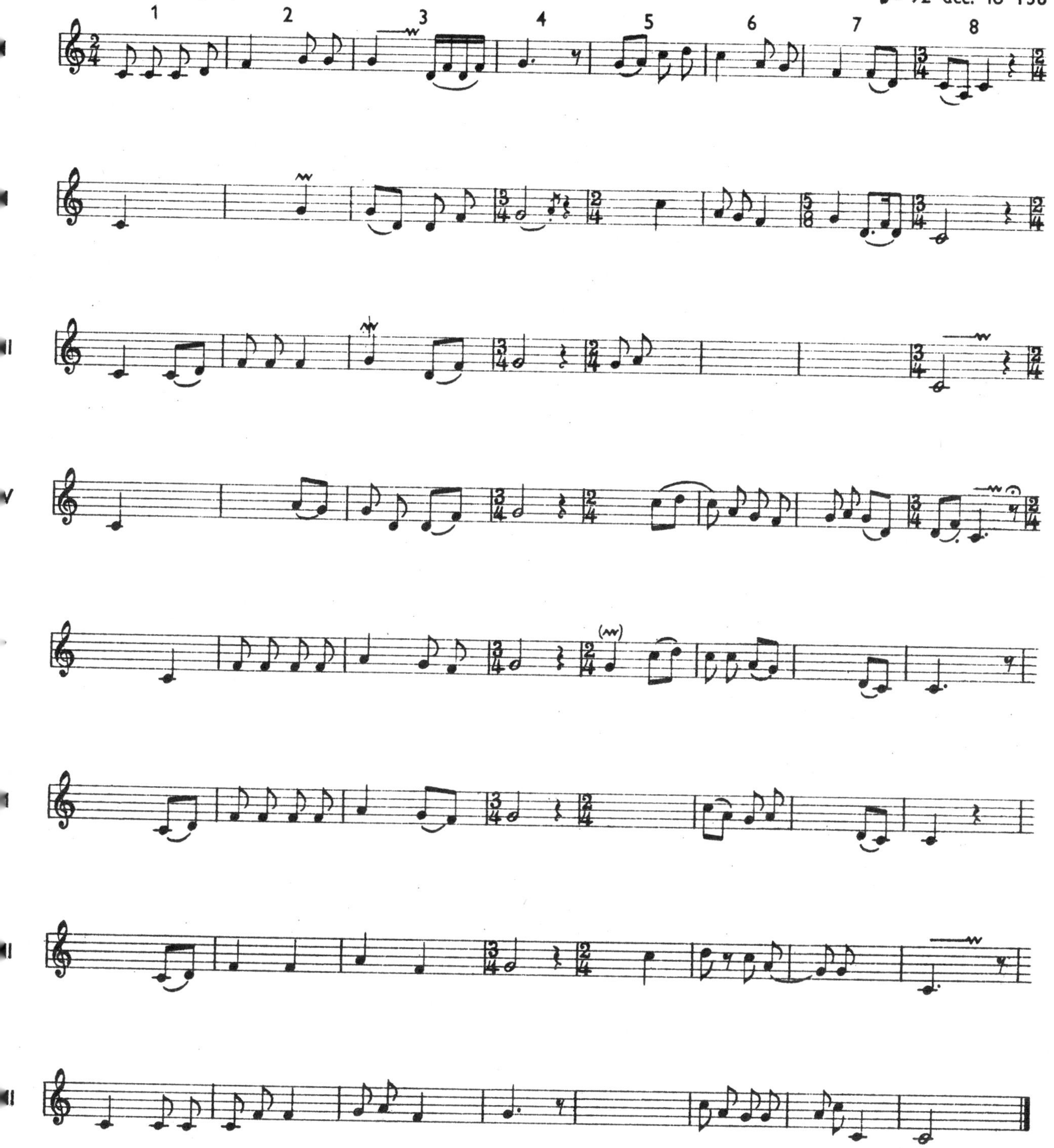

12 Khaguchin manju dagu; shiluk dagu

Old Manchu song; strophic song

Male voice ($c^1\sharp$) ♪=168-176

13 Khaguchin ching ulus manju dagu

Old Manchu song

Male voice (b)

14 Keger morin

The brown horse

Male voice (b)

E

JALAIT

15 Chinggis Khagan-u dagulal

The song of Chingis Khan

Male voice (g)

♩= 112-120

16 Tengri-yin salkin

The winds of heaven

Male voice (f♯)

♩= 11

Record begins in the middle of the verse

17 Danai-bala

Male voice and fiddle

I
fid.
8
9
10
11
12
13
14
II
v.
3
fid.
III
v.
fid.
IV
v.
fid.
tr
V
v.
fid.
tr
VI
v.
fid.
3

15
16
17
18
19
20
21
22

18 Salin öndür

Male voice and fiddle

♩ = 72

8
9
10
11
12
13
14

19 Khan shiu ying

Male voice and fiddle

♪= 144

11
12
13
14
15
16
17
18
19
20
rit.
a tempo
rit.
a tempo
rit.
a tempo
rit.
a tempo

20 *Wang li and Buyan keshik*

Male voice and fiddle

9
10
11
12
13
14
15
16

17
18
19
20
21
22
23
24
I
fid.
II
v.
fid.
III
v.
fid.
IV
v.
fid.
V
v.
fid.

25
26
27
28
29
30
31
32

21 Sang yen noyan-u dagu

The song of prince Sang yen

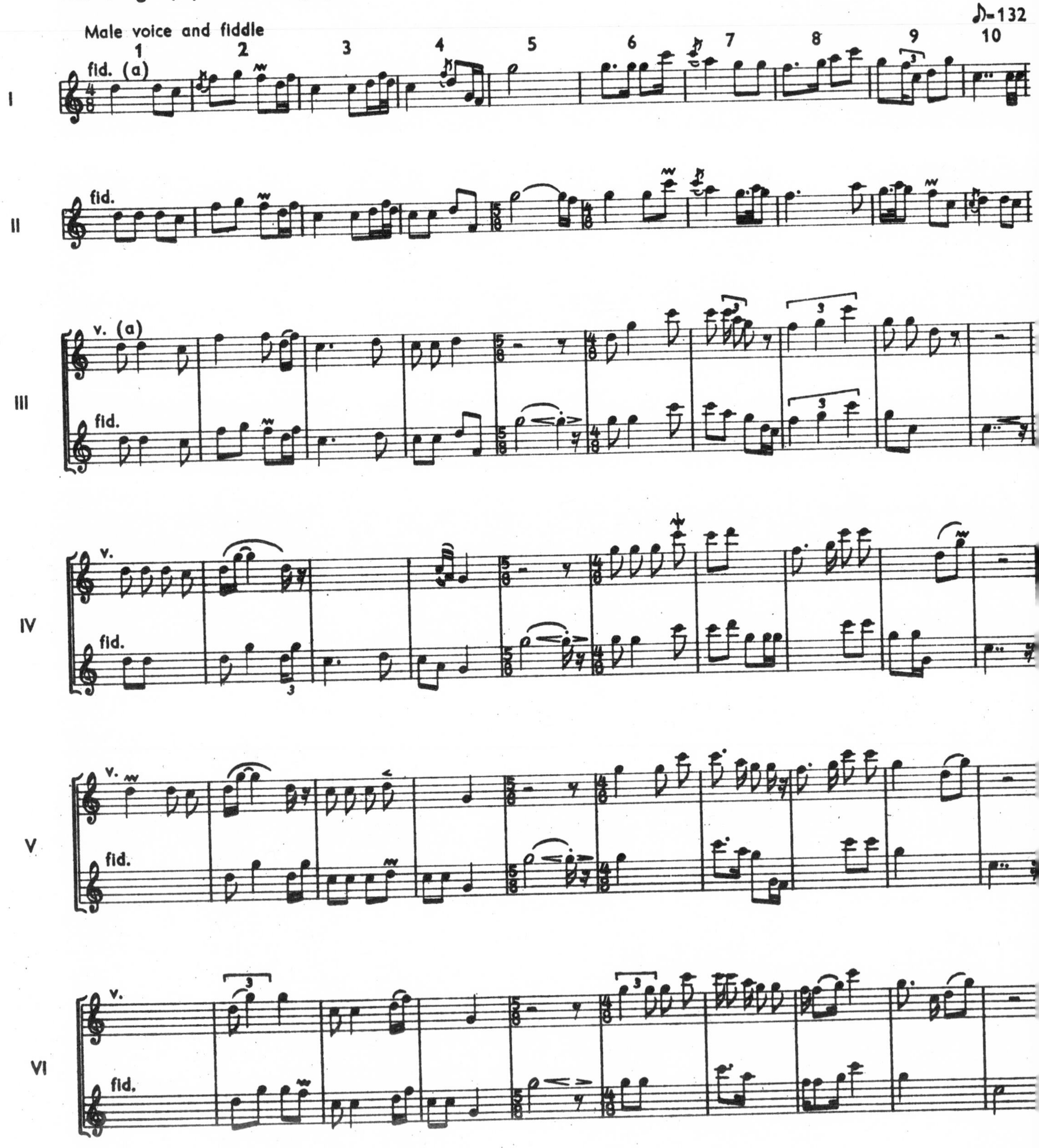

11 12 13 14 15 16 17 18 19 20 21

22 Yerü-yin nagadun-u dagu

A common ditty

Male voice and flute

23 Asaraltu degedüs
The compassionate saints

Male voice and flute

♪ = 126 acc. to 152

24 Dönggör-ün blama

The lama from Dong-kor

Male voice and flute

♪= 132 acc. to 168

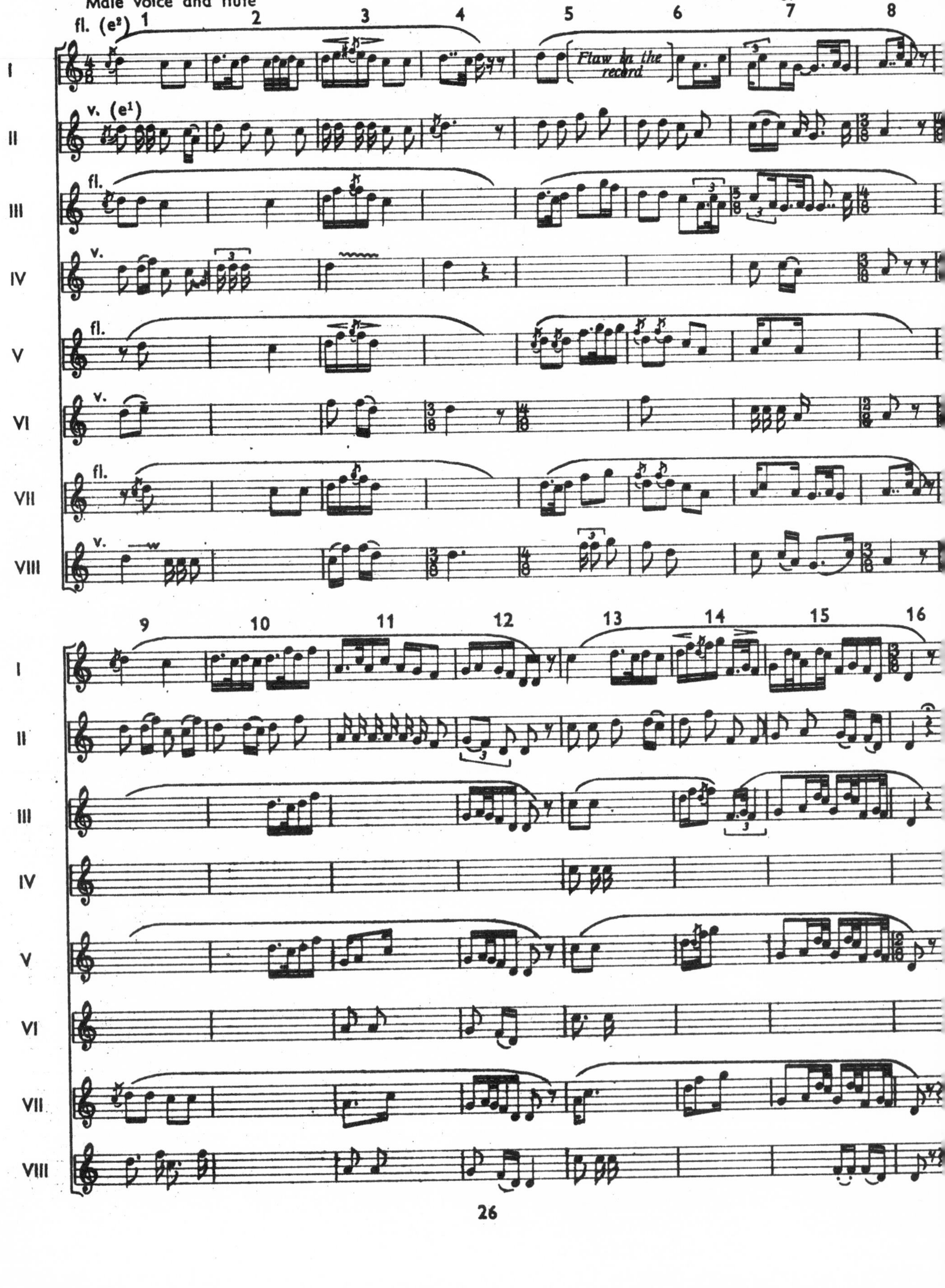

5 Köke tug

The blue banner

Male voice and flute

26 Dönggör-ün blama

The lama from Dong-kor

Male voice and flute

9
10
11
12
13
14
15
16
rit

27 Altan shingkhar

The white falcon *(name of a mountain)*

Male voice and flute

8
9
10
11
12
13
14

1
2
3
4
5
6
7
fl.
v.
XI
XII
XIII
XIV
XV
XVI
XVII
XVIII
XIX

8
9
10
11
12
13
14
Flaw in the record
Record breaks off.

28 Male voice and flute

♩=92

9
10
11
12
13
14
15
16
17

F

KHORCHIN

29 Önnge saitu tolin-dur

In the beautiful mirror

♩= 60

30 Abu Chinggis

Our ancestor Chingis Khan

♩= 96

31 Toktogu

♪= 112 acc. to 132

2 Shui shu

♩= 92

3 Jegün agula

The eastern mountain

♩= 80

4 Mansushiri

Manjusri

♩= 76

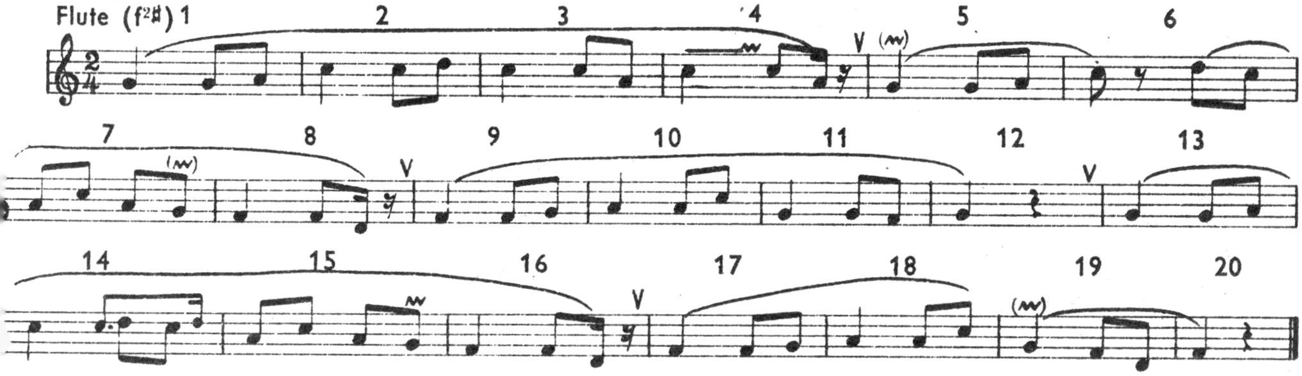

35 Urida ebüge Chinggis Khagan-u bagatur chirig-ün daguu

Song of the warriors of Chingis Khan, our ancestor of old

Male voice with zither and guitar

♩= 84

9
10
11
12
13
14
15
16

1
2
3
4
5
6
7
8
v.
zt.
gt.
VI
VII
VIII
IX

9
10
11
12
13
14
15
16

36 *The song of the four seasons* (Khaguchin daguulal — *an old song*)

Male voice with zither and guitar

♩= 126

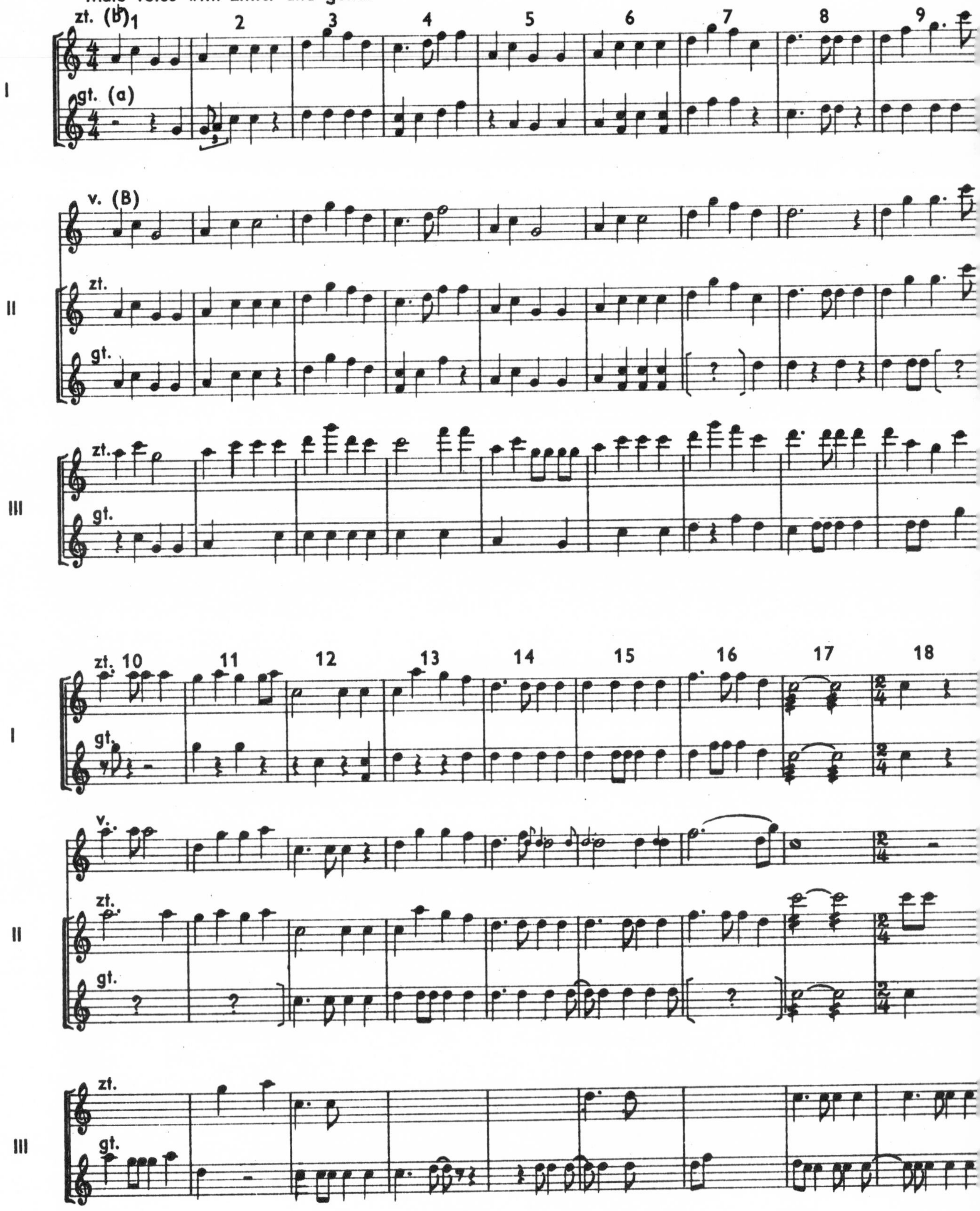

37 Tümen jil-ün chichik

The flowers of a thousand years

Fiddle (b♭) ♪= 152

38 Tengsel ügei

Incomparable

Two male voices (g) ♩= 72 acc. to 80

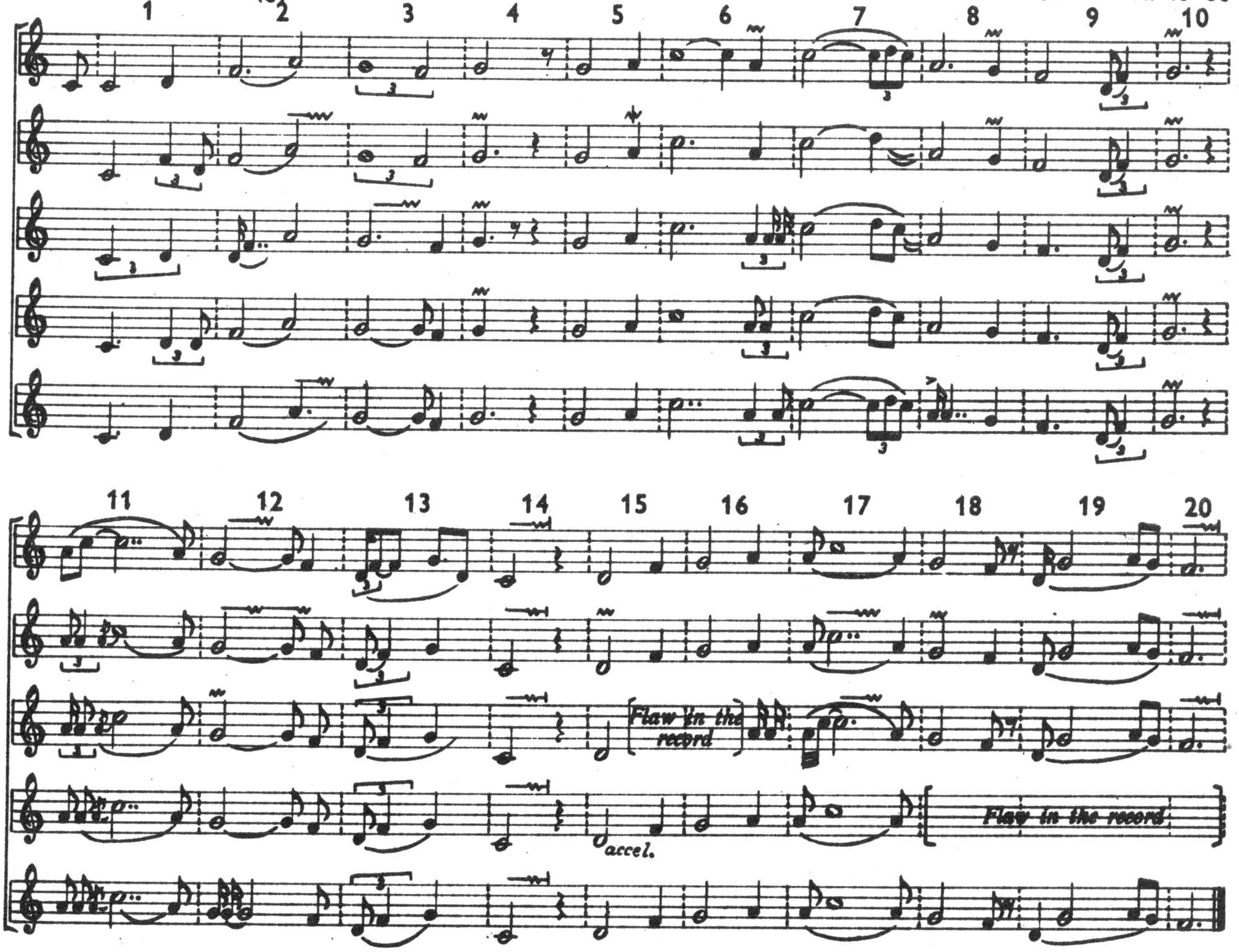

39 Bogdo Namba

Holy Namba

Two male voices (b)

♪=(80

I II III IV

40 Bogdo Namba

Holy Namba

Two flutes (d²)

♪=(116

I II III IV

I
II
III
IV
I
II
III
IV

KHORCHIN JASAKTU

41 Küji utaga

The smoke of incense

Female voice (f^1)

♩=6

42

Male voice (e)

♪= 100 acc. to 16

43 Arban Sain

The ten good things

♩=6

Chorus (c#)

44 Abu Chinggis

Our ancestor Chingis Khan

Ten male voices (d#)

♩= 72 acc. to 1

5 Öndür degere-eche

Down from the height

Female voice (b♭)

46 Ba se ling noyan-i üdeksen daguulal

Song to accompany prince Pa-szu-ling

Male voice (a) ♪=12

47 Khotala buyantu monggol

All brave Mongols

Male voice (a) ♪= 13

48 Uruskhu Togor gool-un usu tunggalak

The waters of the running Togur river are limpid

Ten male voices (d^1) ♪= 11

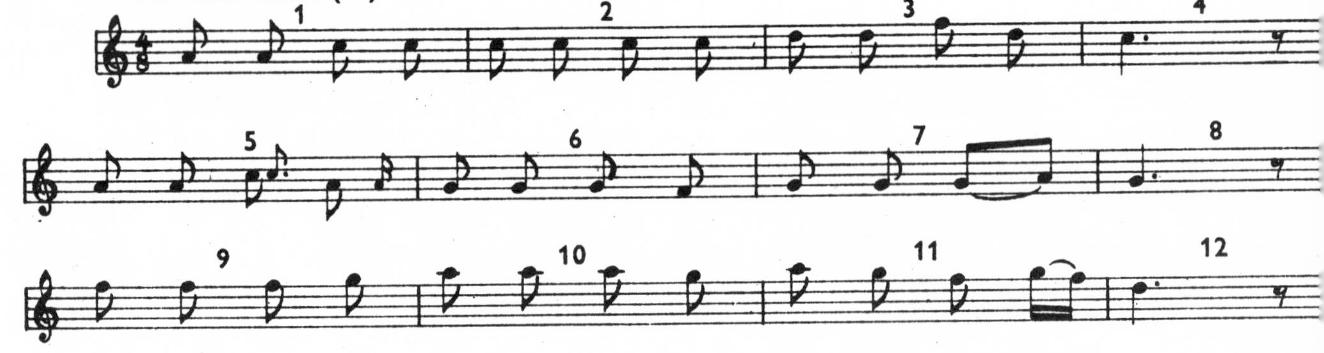

49 Monggol-iyan manduguikhu daguulal

Eight male voices (f¹) ♪= 78 acc. to 152

50 El guniyang

Male voice and fiddle ♩= 88

51 Shi lau

Male voice and fiddle

♪=132

11
12
13
14
15
16
17
18
19
20

52 Gangraiman

Male voice and fiddle

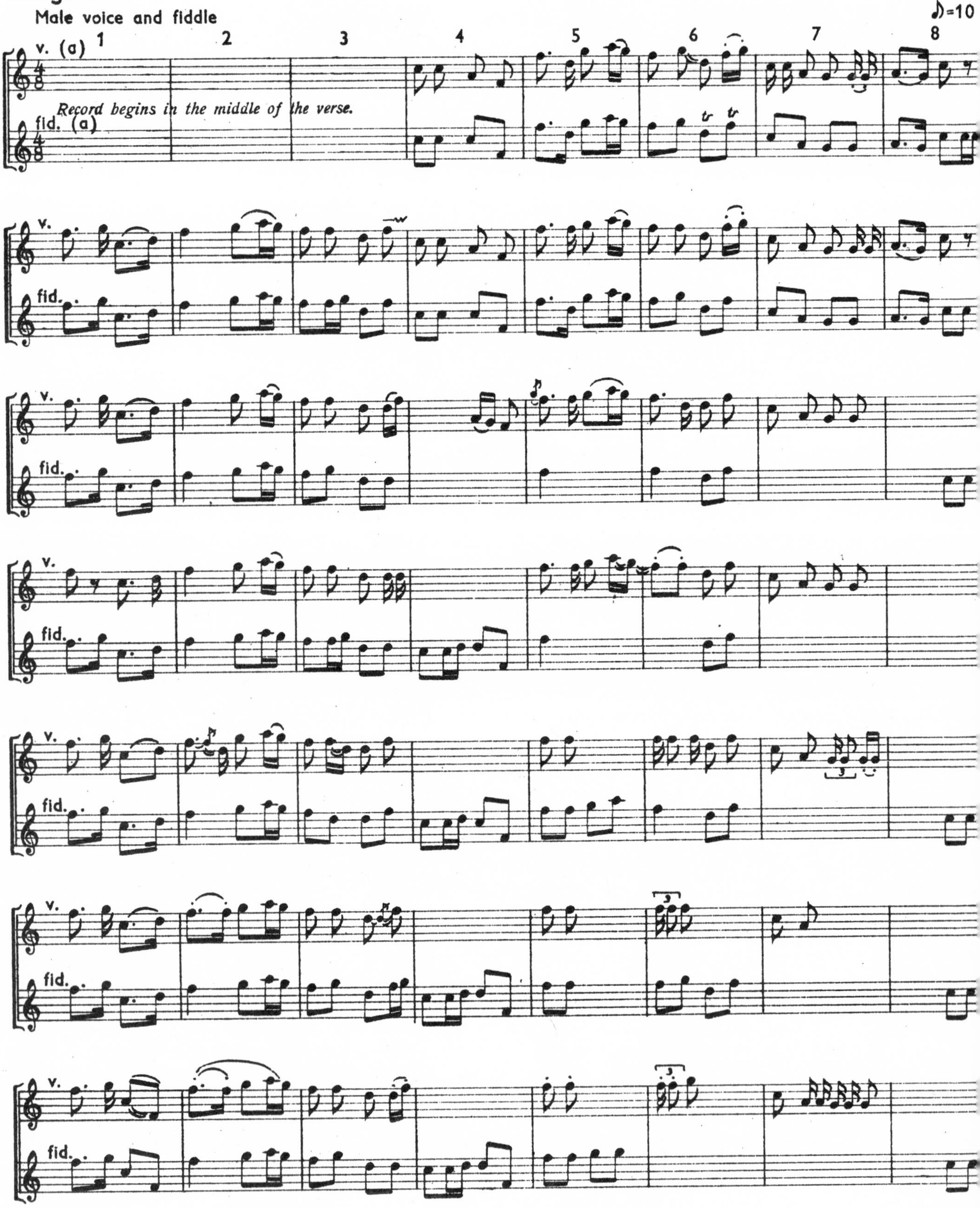

9
10
11
12
13
14
15
16

53 Khan shao ing

Male voice with fiddle and guitar ♪=192

1 2 3 4 5 6 7 8 9 10
v.
gt.
VI
VII
VIII
IX
(!)
X

Record breaks off.

54 Khasar Chinggis, Jasaktu-yin guchin shilük

Khasar Chingis; the thirty stanzas of Jasaktu

♩= (84

Two male voices (b)

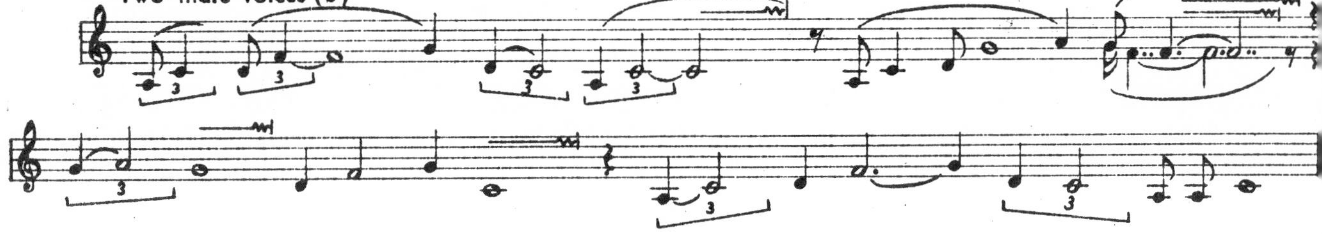

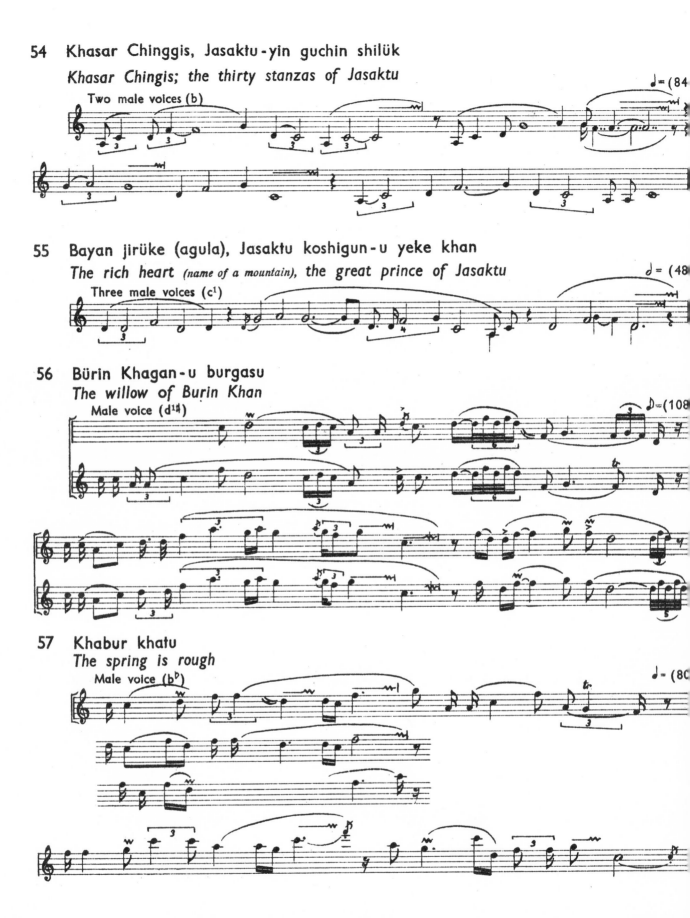

55 Bayan jirüke (agula), Jasaktu koshigun-u yeke khan

The rich heart (name of a mountain), the great prince of Jasaktu

𝅗𝅥= (48

Three male voices (c[1])

56 Bürin Khagan-u burgasu

The willow of Burin Khan

♪= (108

Male voice (d[1]♯)

57 Khabur khatu

The spring is rough

♩= (80

Male voice (b♭)

59 Bolor-un gegegen naran

The sun bright as crystal

Male voice (e^1) ♩=(80)

60 Narin köke morin

The slim blue horse

61 Mesheri

62 Naran shikür

The sun-shade

63 Naiman agula

The eight mountains

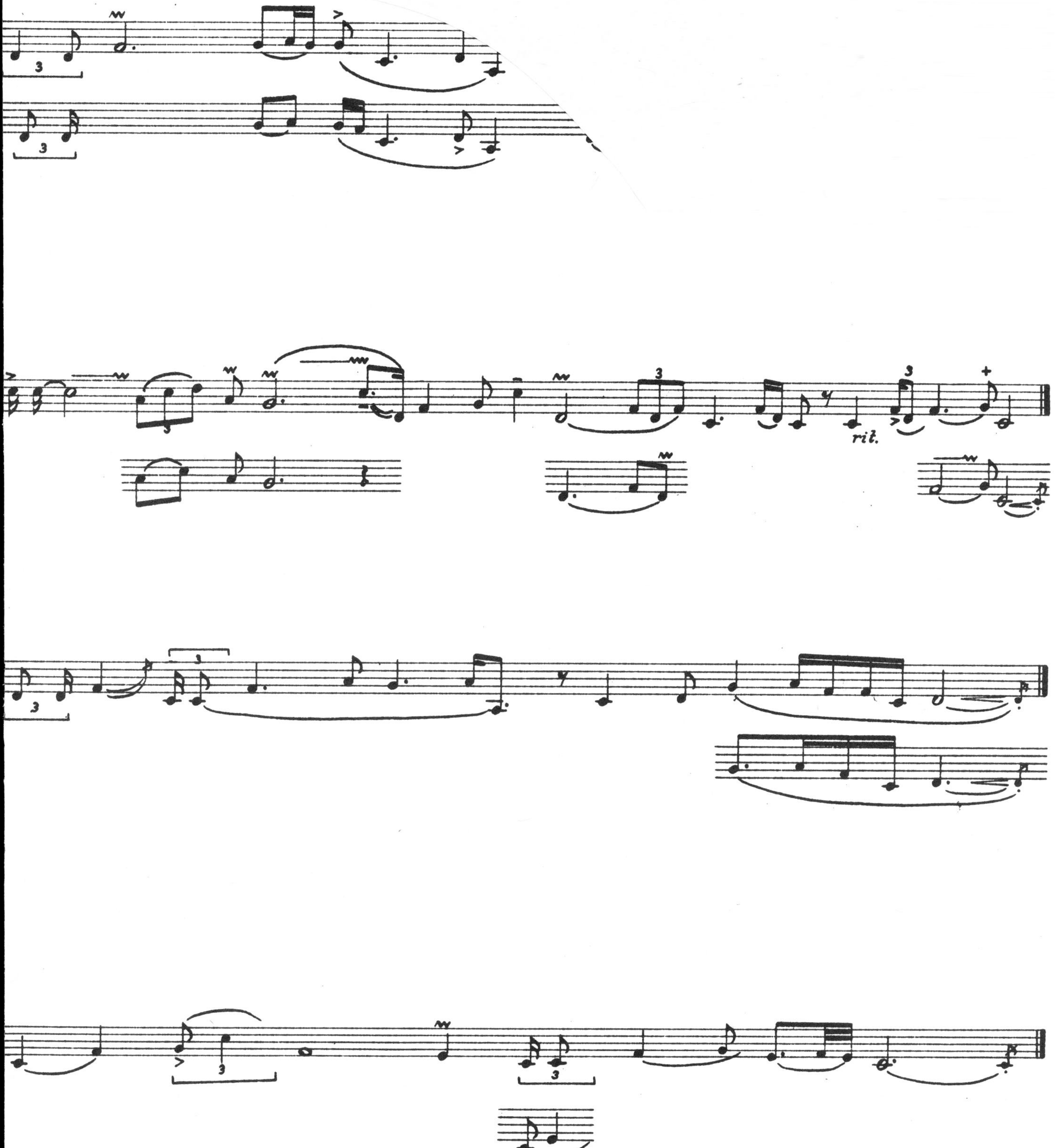
rit.

64 Kürüng joro

The fallow ambler

Female voice (c^{2})

65 Sukha khoyar modo

The two sukha-trees

Two voices, male and female (d^{1})

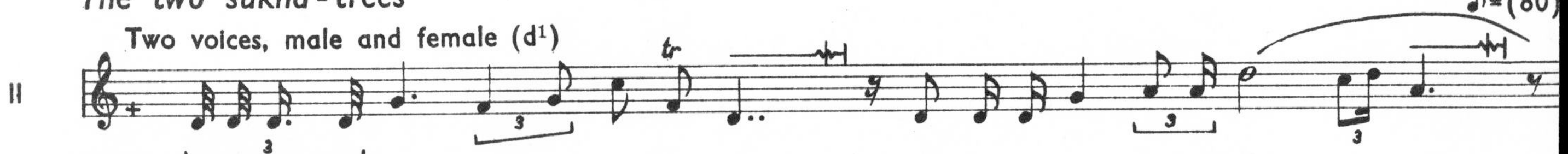

66 Yaklai baga

Little Yaglai

Male voice (c^{1}♯)

67 Khotala buyantu monggol

All brave Mongols

Male voice (a)

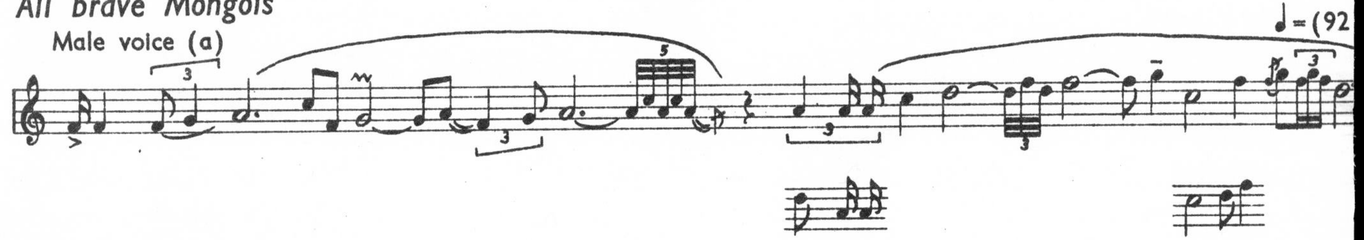

68 Naiman tib

The eight parts of the world

Male voice (a)

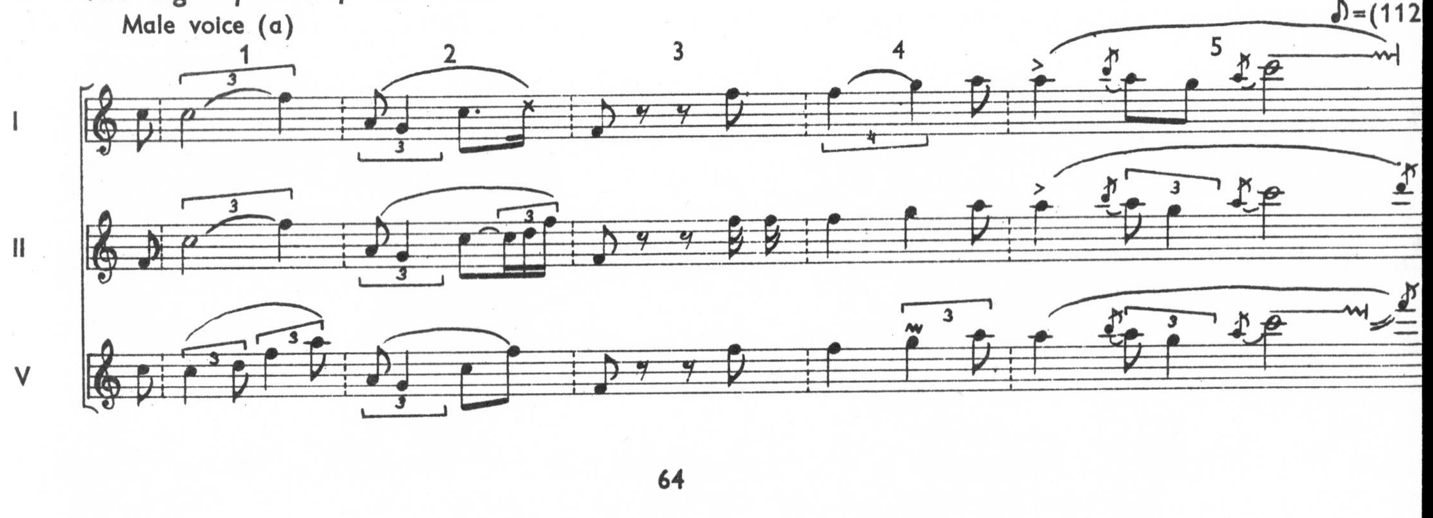

falsetto
rit.
6
7
8
9

69

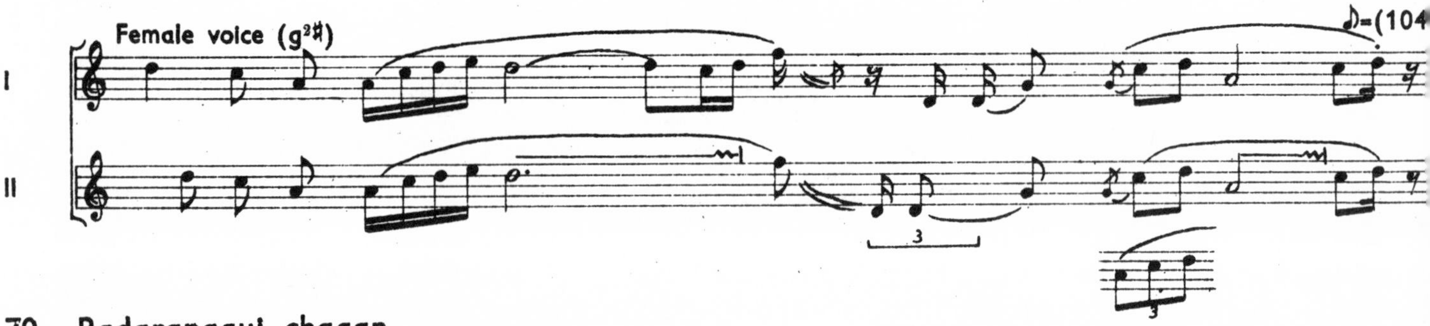

70 Badaranggui chagan

Dazzlingly white

71 Chimed Badma

8 9 10 11 12 13 14 15
rit.
11 12 13 14 15 16 17 18 19

G GORLOS

72 Ümü chiyü dzangdang

Male voice and two fiddles ♩=100

H TUMET

73 Jangshur angga

♩=72 acc. to 84

Male voice and fiddle

I BARIN

74 Damru khadan-u aru

North of the drum-rock

Male voice (b) ♪=(104)

9 10 11 12 13 14 15 16 17
Record breaks off.

6 7 8 9 10 11

K

KHARCHIN

75 **Khuduk dotora baikhu khoisha melekei**

The grey (?) frog in the well

Male voice with flute and guitar

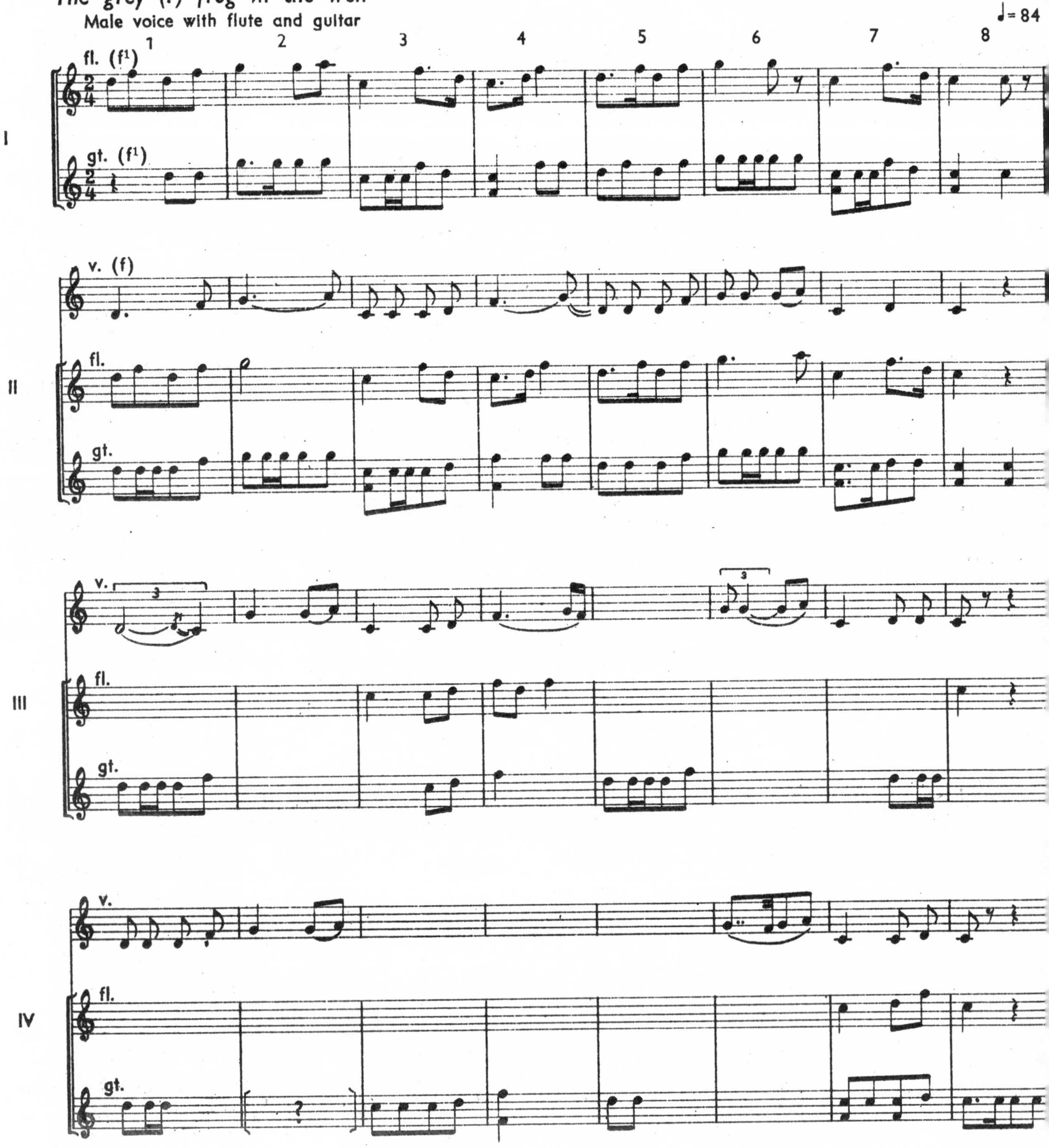

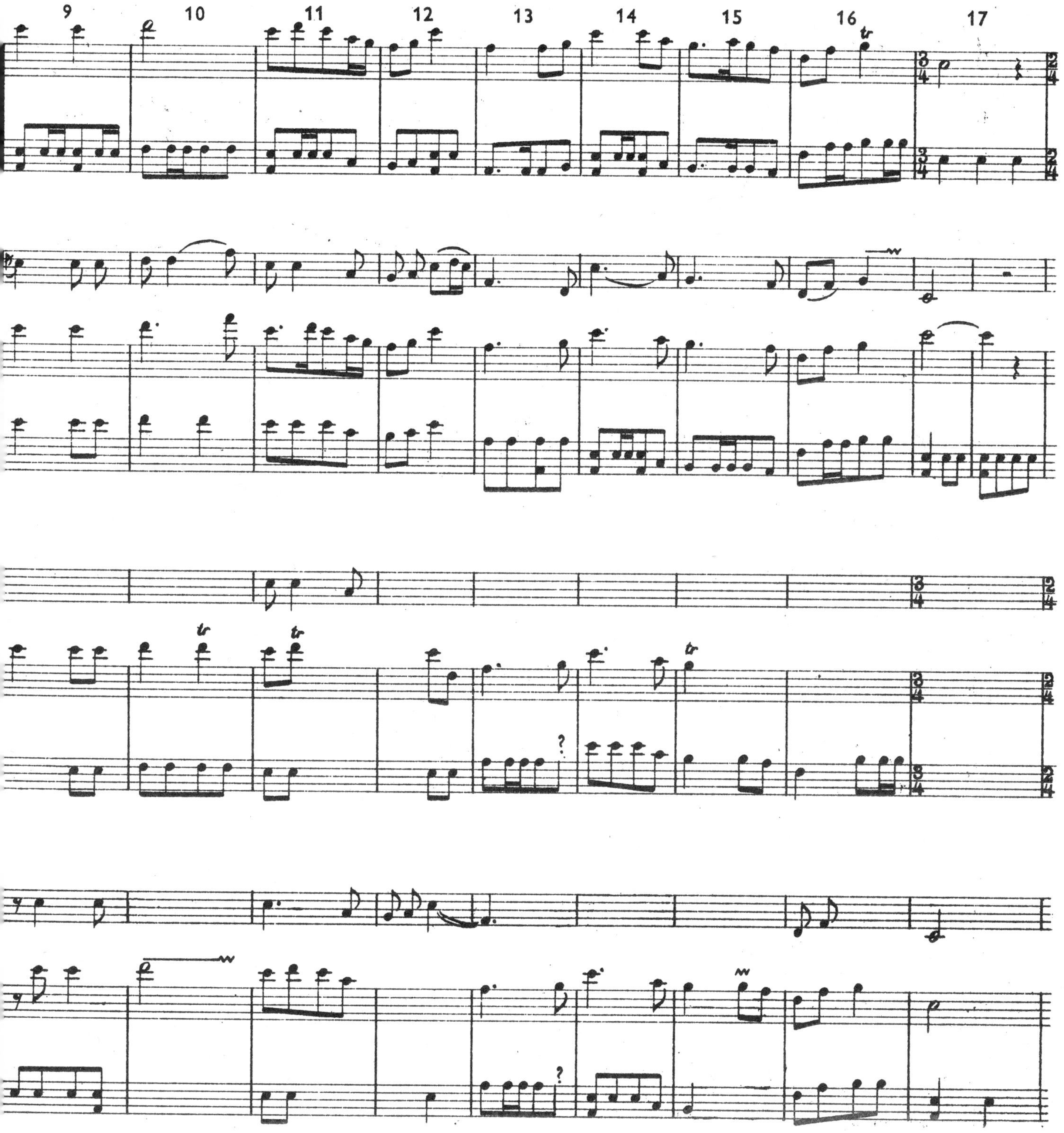
9
10
11
12
13
14
15
16
17
tr

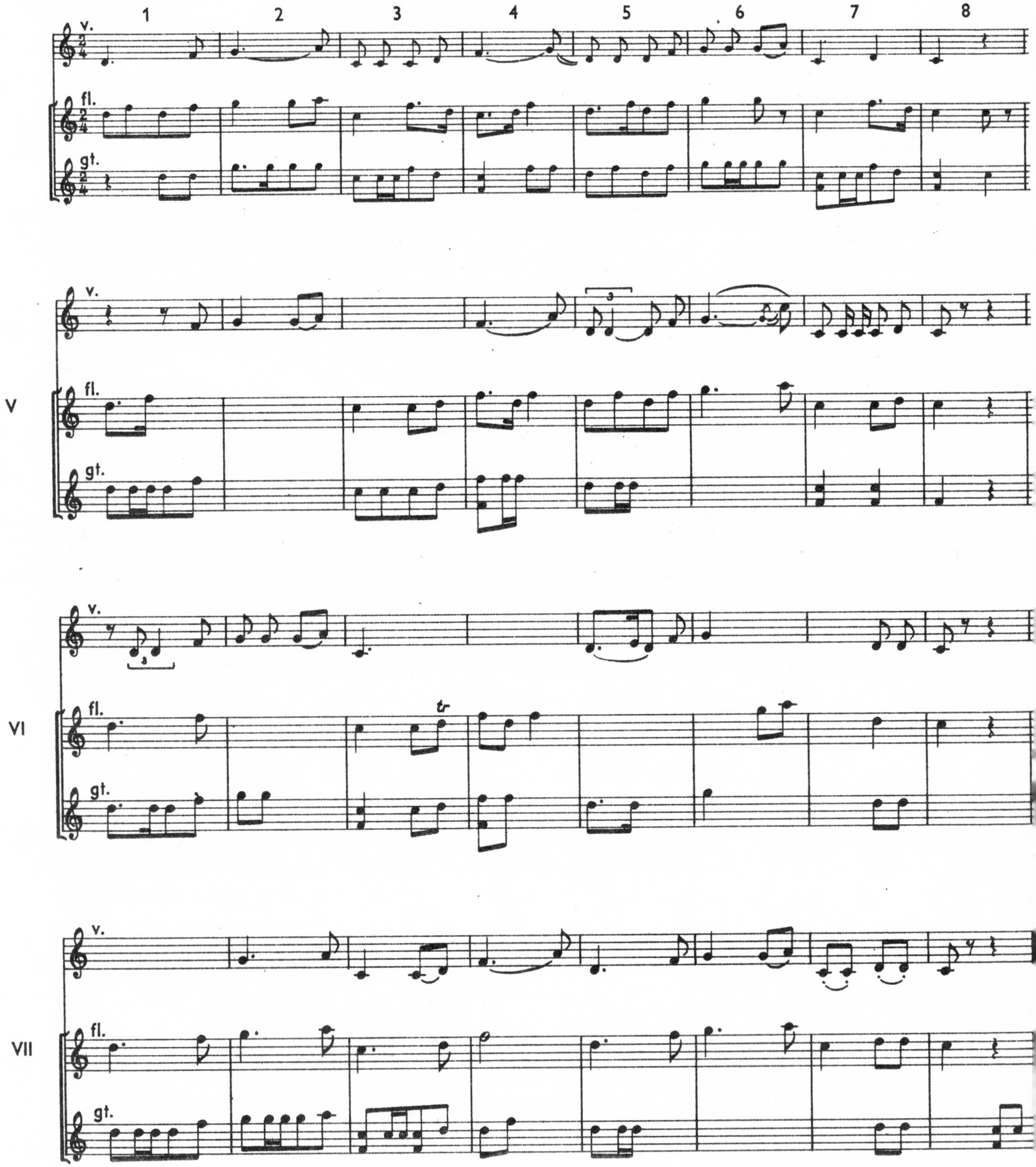
1 2 3 4 5 6 7 8
v.
fl.
gt.
V
VI
VII
tr

9
10
11
12
13
14
15
16
17

76 Kharchin duu

A Kharchin song

Male voice with fiddle and guitar

♩= 126

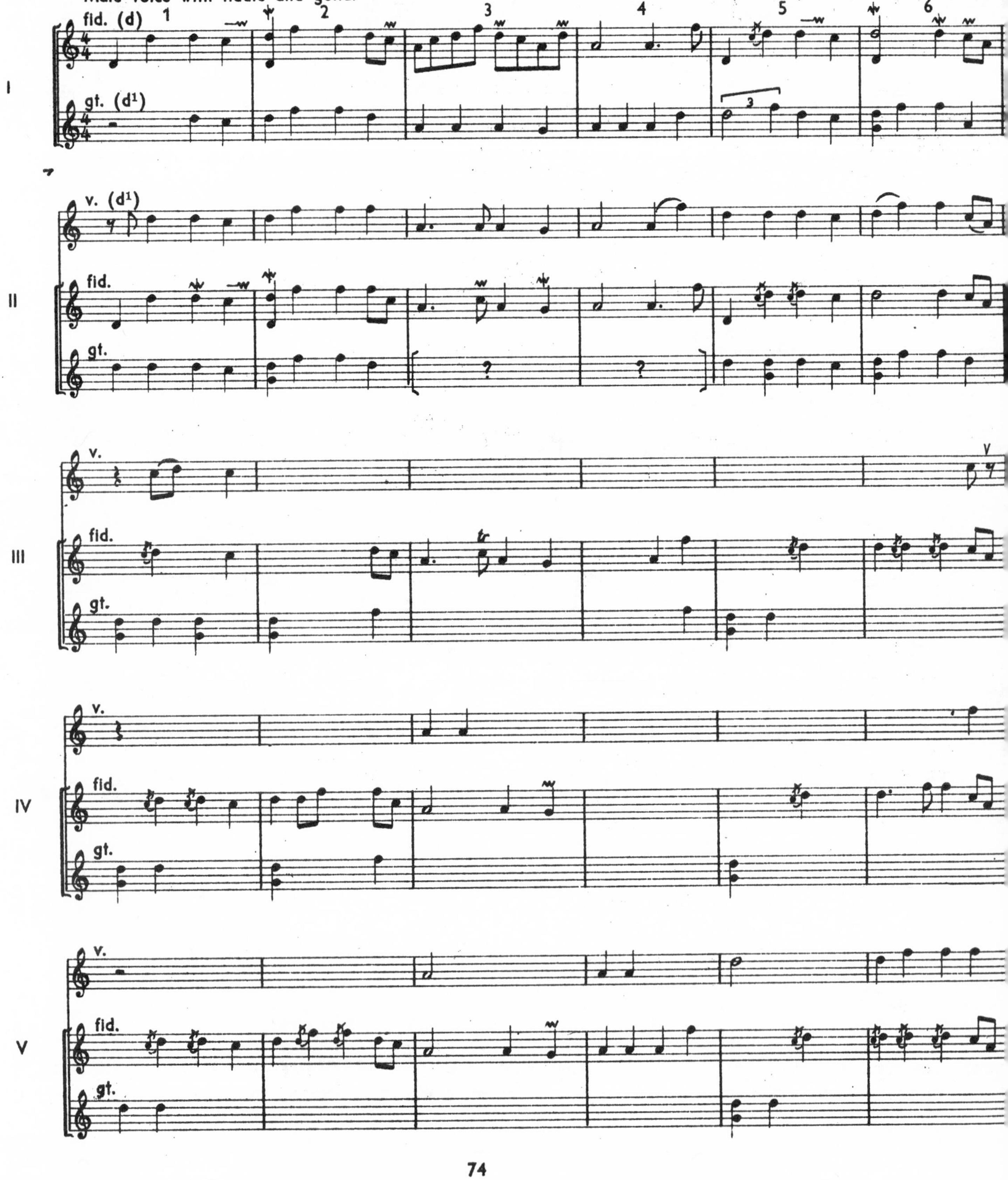

7
8
9
10
11
12
13

14
15
16
17
18
19
20
I
fid.
gt.
II
v.
fid.
gt.
III
v.
fid.
gt.
IV
v.
fid.
gt.
ritard.
V
v.
fid.
gt.

7 Dung shan

The eastern mountain

Male voice with fiddle and guitar ♩= 84

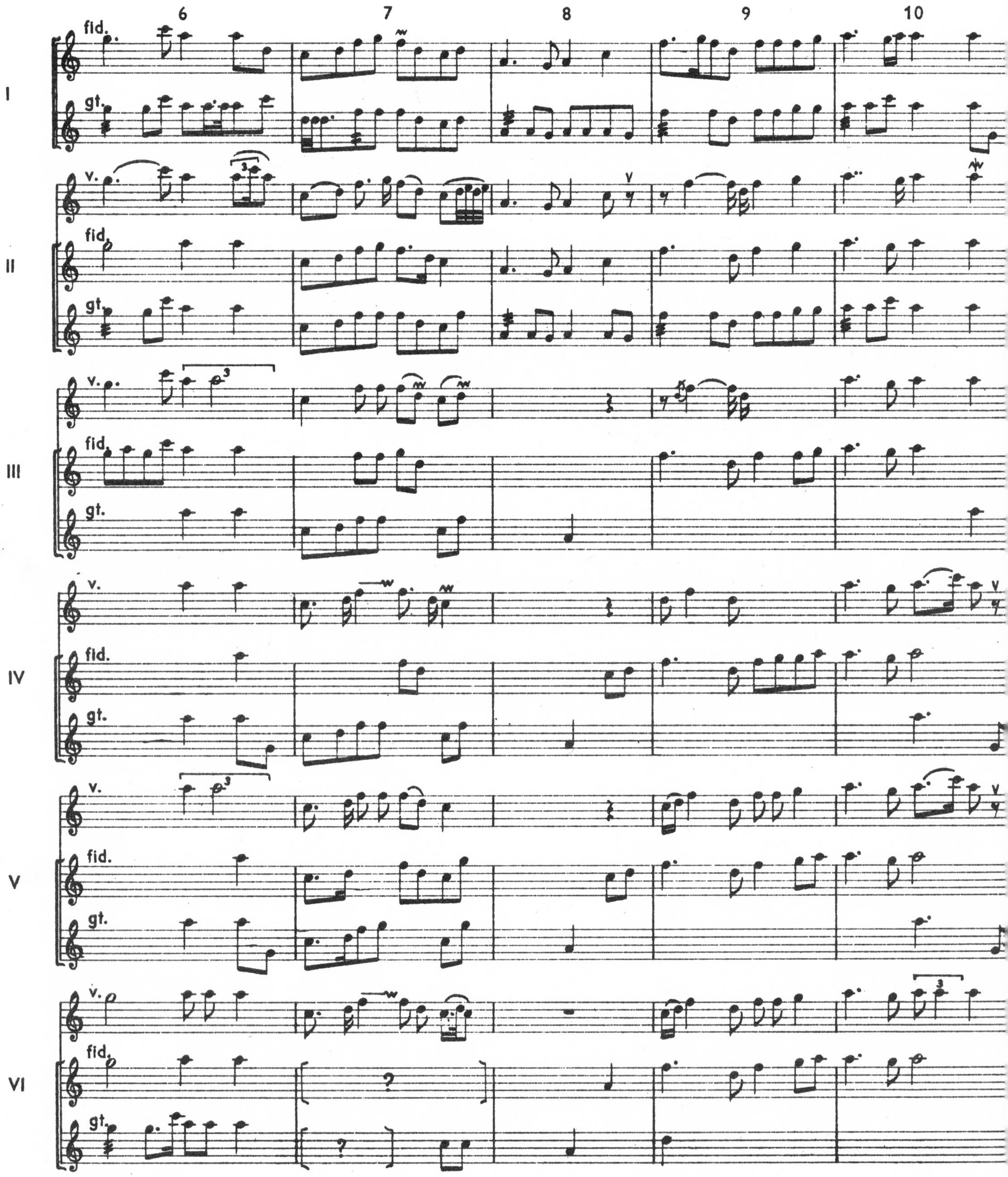
6
7
8
9
10
fid.
gt.
I
v.
fid.
II
gt.
v.
fid.
III
gt.
v.
fid.
IV
gt.
v.
fid.
V
gt.
v.
fid.
VI
gt.

11
12
13
14
15
16

L

CHAHAR

78 Kögerükei

Two voices, male and female, with fiddle and guitar

♩= 108 acc. to 152

8
9
10
11
12
13
14
15
rit.
accel.
accel.
rit.
rit.
rit.
accel.

79 Chakhar naiman khoshigu

The eight banners of Chahar

80 Monggol-un nairatai

81 Kögerükei

M 1 HAILAR

82 Shilük dagu

Strophic song

Male voice (b) ♩= 80

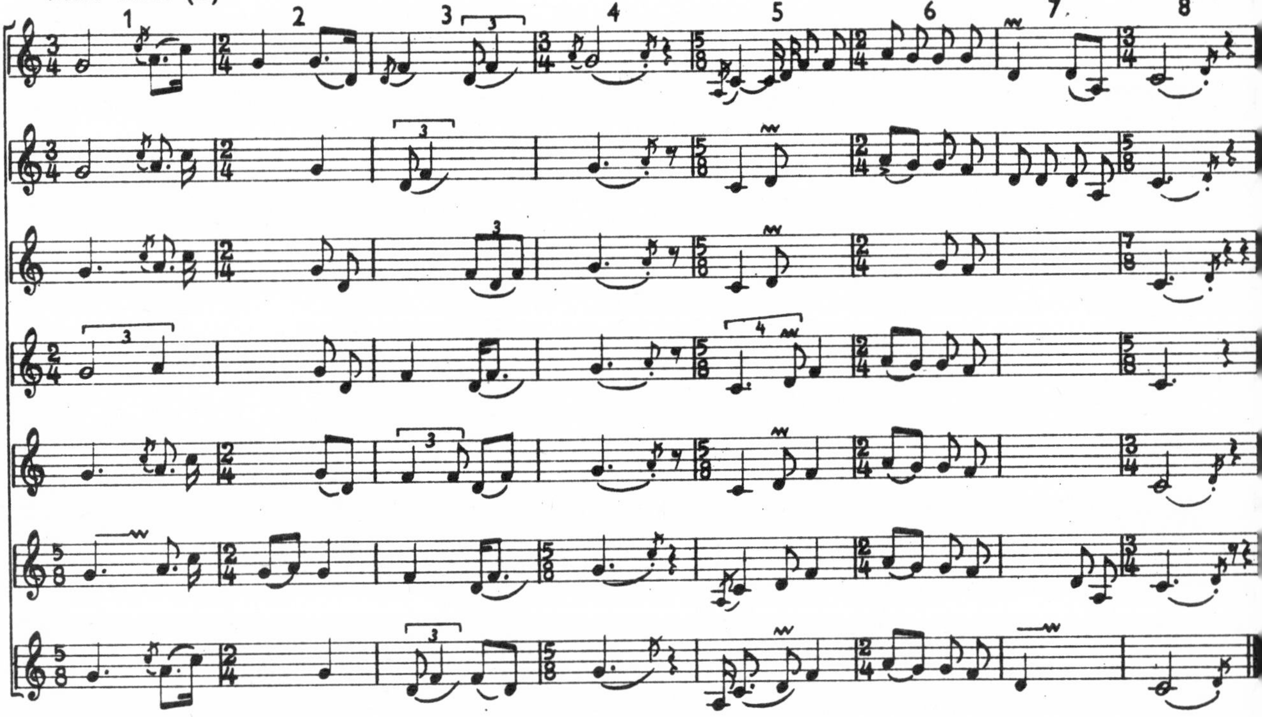

83 Onon gool-un ikhe-yin gargaksan dagu

Song of the Great from the Onon river

Male voice (g♯) ♪= 160

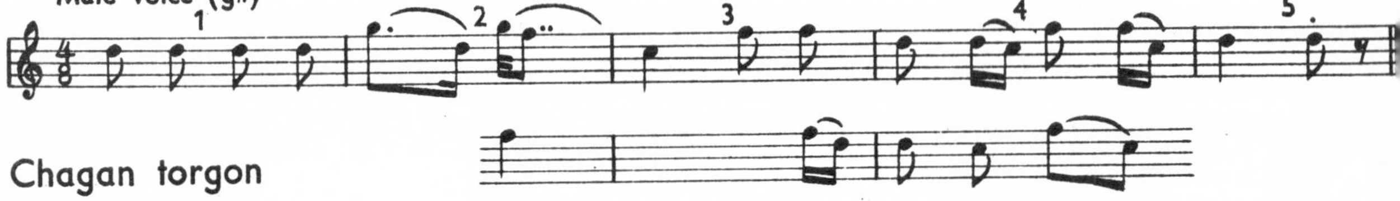

84 Chagan torgon

The white silk

Male voice (g) ♩= 80

35 Arban khan

The ten kings

Male voice (e)

♪ = 168

86 **Chagan torgon**

The white silk

87 **Manju ulus-un chirig-un dagu**

The soldiers' song of the Manchu nation

88 **Ulus baiguluksan dagu**

The song of the establishment of a people

M 2 HSINKING

89 **Badma lingkhua chichik**

The lotus flower

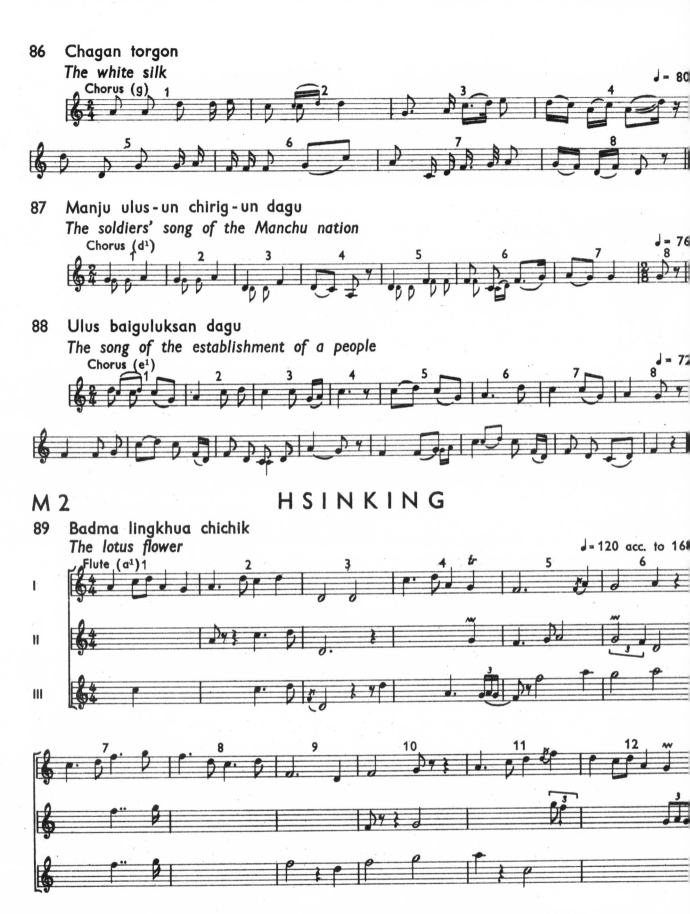

90 *Old Mongol tune*

91 *Old Mongol tune*

5
6
7
8
9
♩=100

5
6
7
8
9

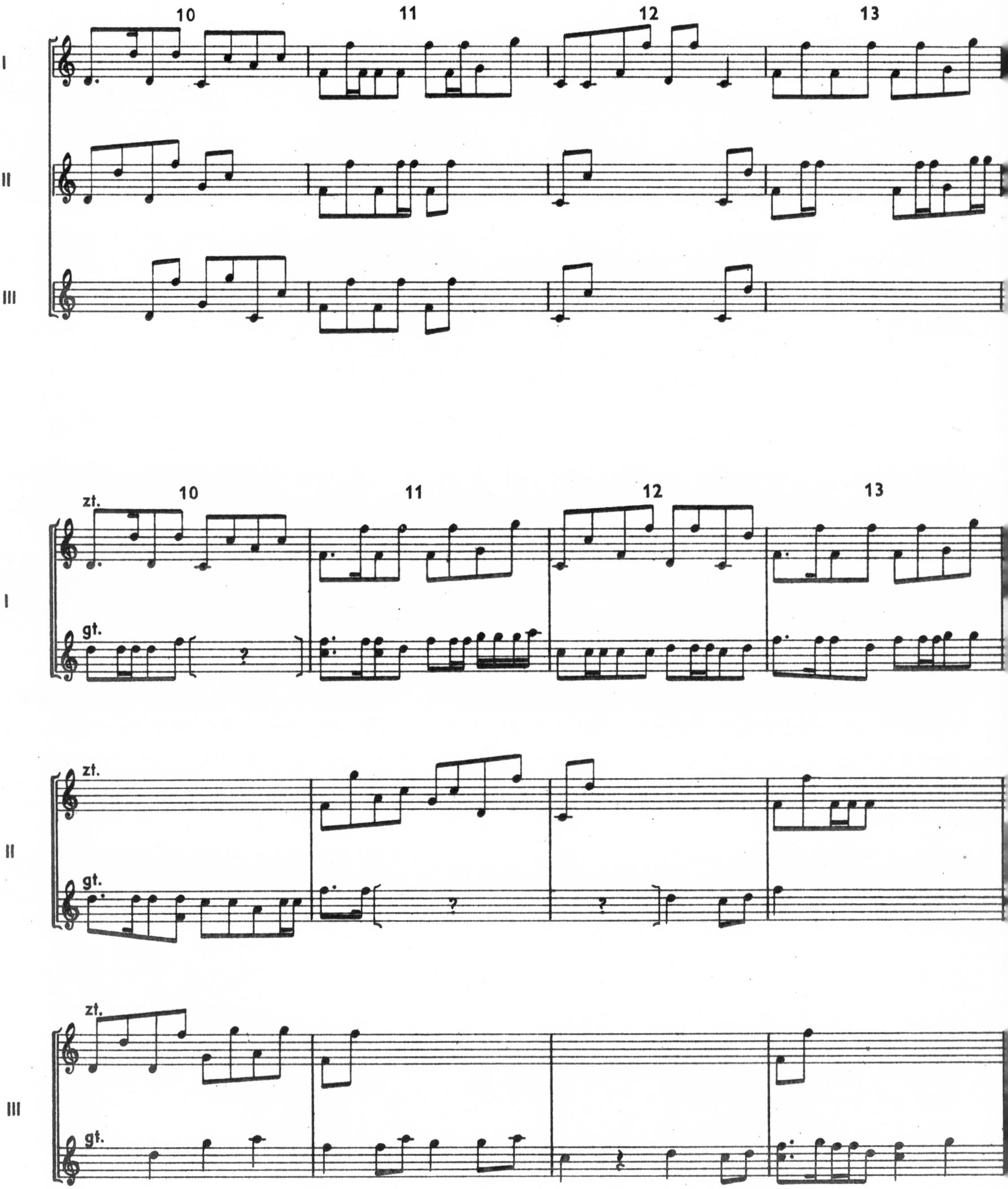
10
11
12
13
I
II
III
zt.
gt.

14
15
16
17
112
accel.
14
15
16
17

18
19
20
21
I
II
♩= 126
III
zt.
gt.

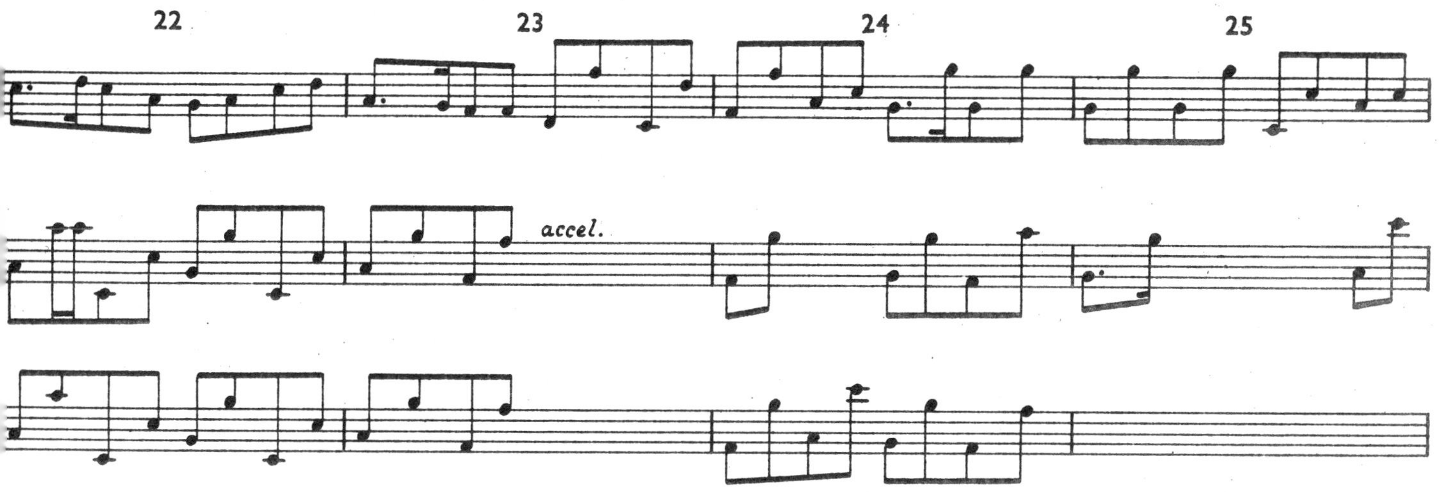
22
23
24
25
accel.

22
23
24
25

26
27
28
29
I
♩=138
accel.
II
III

26
27
28
29
zt.
gt.
I
zt.
gt.
II
zt.
gt.
III

30
31
32
33

30
31
32
33

34
35
36
37
I
II
III
♩=152
accel.

34
35
36
37
I
II
III
zt.
gt.

38
39
40
41
ritardando
38
39
40
41
